# Magic Pickle

## and the Creature from the Black Legume

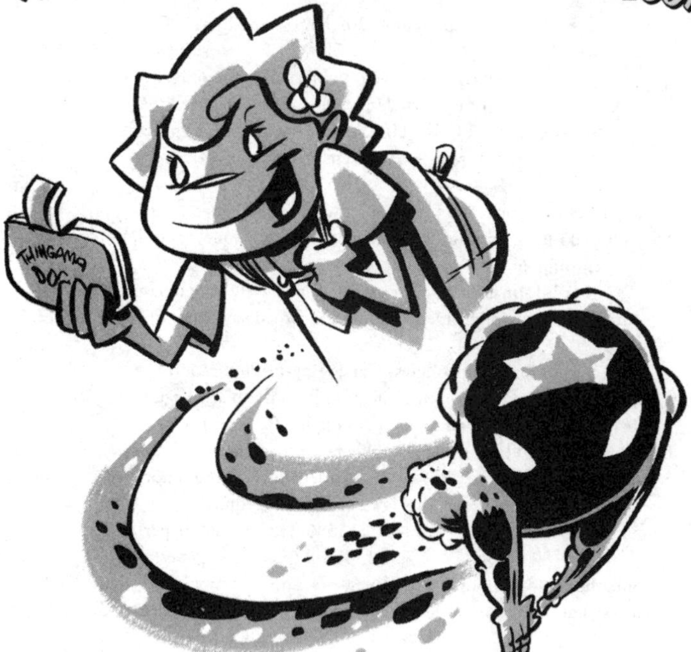
THINGAMA DOG

By Scott Morse

A graphix Chapter Book

An imprint of
SCHOLASTIC
New York Toronto London Auckland Sydney Mexico City New Delhi Hong Kong

Library of Congress Cataloging-in-Publication Data
Morse, Scott. Magic Pickle and the Creature from the Black Legume / by Scott Morse.
— 1st ed. p. cm. "A Graphix Chapter Book."
Summary: When Jo Jo and Magic Pickle face off against a bad legume during a class
field trip to a peanut factory, it is not the fearless dill superhero nor his video game that
save the day but Jo Jo's ingenuity.
ISBN-13: 978-0-545-13886-4 (pbk. : alk. paper),
ISBN-10: 0-545-13886-8 (pbk. : alk. paper)
[1. Superheroes—Fiction. 2. Vegetables—Fiction. 3. School field trips—Fiction. 4.
Video games—Fiction. 5. Humorous stories.] I. Title. PZ7.M84642Mac 2009
[Fic]—dc22 2009009043

10 9 8 7 6 5 4 3 2 1      09 10 11 12 13

First edition, September 2009

Printed in the U.S.A.   23
Edited by Sheila Keenan
Creative Director: David Saylor
Book design by Charles Kreloff

# Prologue

## (or everything you need to know before you read this book)

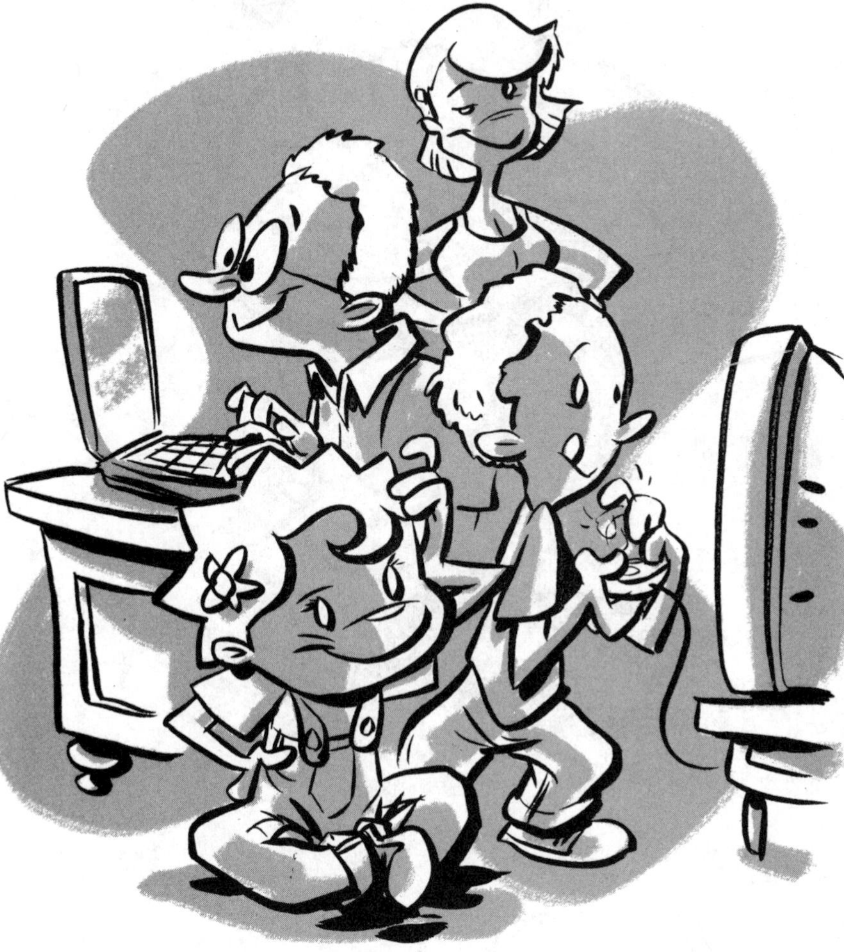

**J**o Jo Wigman was a lot like any normal girl you'd meet in class. She had a pretty great dad who helped add the appeal to his company, Top Banana Computers. She had a pretty great mom who made every day feel like a sunny Sunday (and made a pretty good *ice cream sundae,* too!). Jo Jo's brother, Jason, was nuttier than the nuts on top of *any* sundae, but she put up with him.

The trick was the roommate Jo Jo had living under her bedroom floor.

A "roommate" that no one knew about but *her*.

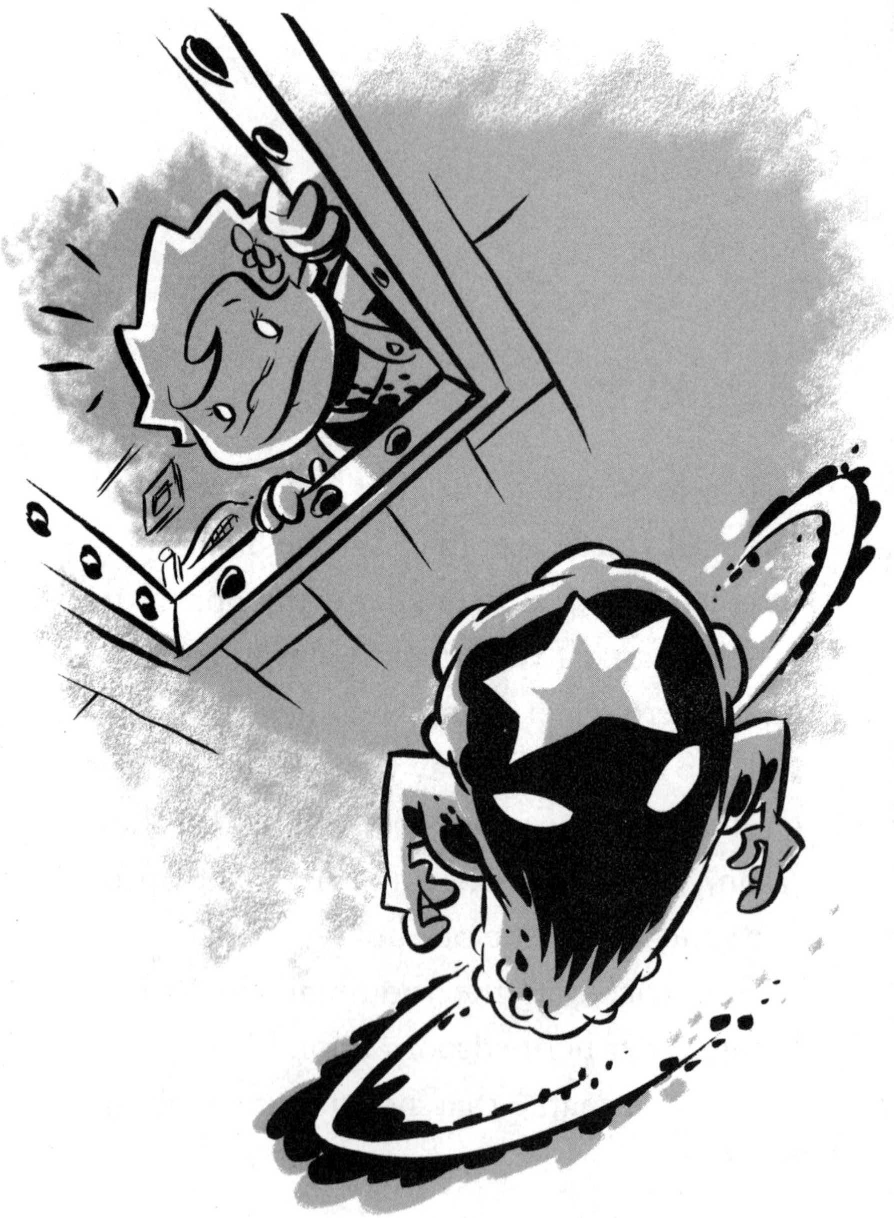

A super-powered secret hero.

An agent of dill justice.

# A pickle . . . a *talking* pickle!

As a government agent, his code name was Weapon Kosher, but that just sounded too darn official, so Jo Jo called him the Magic Pickle. His powers weren't actually magical; they were the result of an experiment gone sour in the Capital Dill lab. (Capital Dill was so secret that the government built a whole town on top of it—and Jo Jo's bedroom was right above the Dill!)

Anyhow, down in the Dill, Dr. Jekyll Formaldehyde was trying to create a special agent of justice to fight crime and keep the world safe from rotten villains.

He was also eating lunch.

A pickle fell into the experiment and . . .

# KAZZZZORK!!!

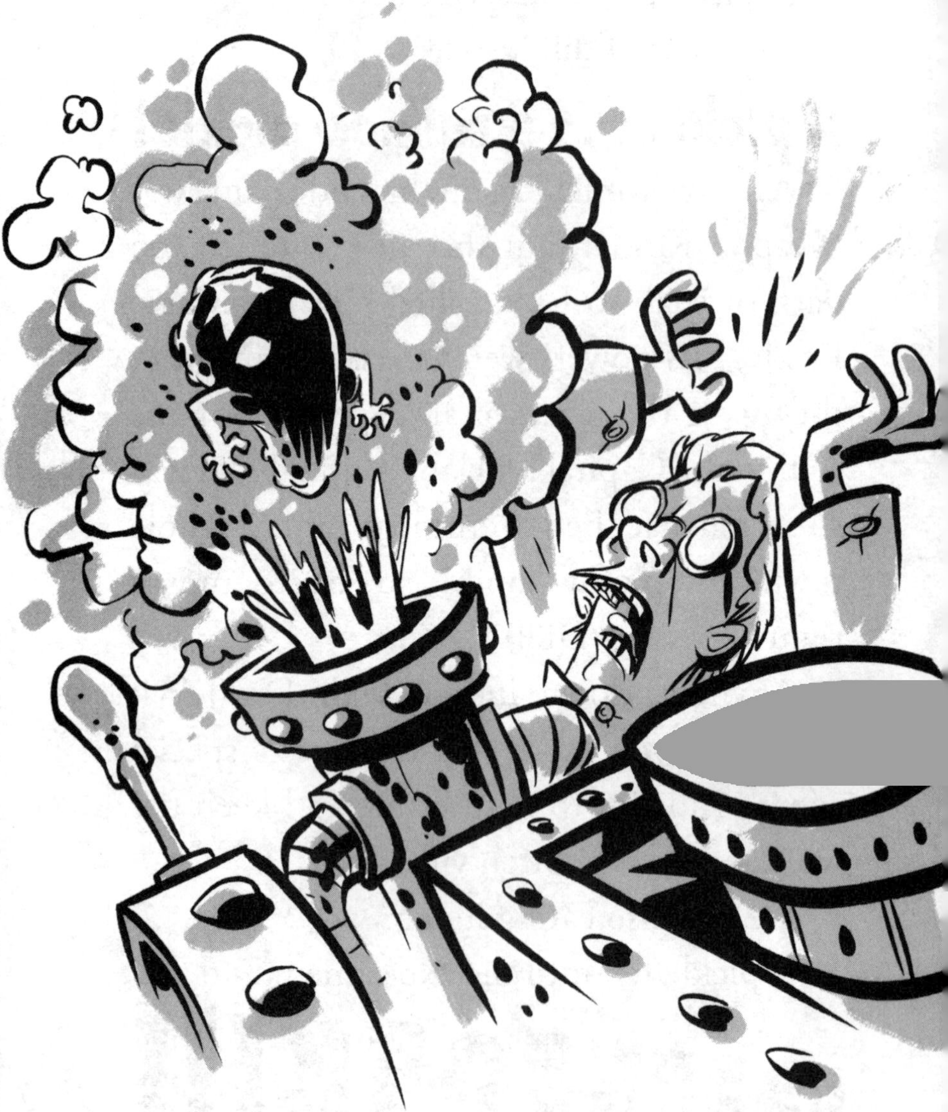

Weapon Kosher was born—but so was something else. . . .

The good doctor's vegetarian combo lunch went *bad* when the radon rays from the gamma particle confibulator struck the veggies!

Dr. Formaldehyde had accidentally created **The Brotherhood of Evil Produce**! The Brotherhood had only one goal: to take over the world and bring forth the Salad Days, a new age in which fruits and veggies would reign over humankind, forcing people to find some other food group to balance their diets. Now it was up to Dr. F.'s kosher dill cohort to save the world.

And that's how Jo Jo came to meet the hush-hush, top-secret, relish-flinging,

fast-flying Weapon Kosher, who burst up through her bedroom floor. They decided to team up. (Okay, there was some debate about it. Okay, okay, *Jo Jo* decided, and she had to talk the Magic Pickle into it.) Girl and pickle worked together to fight the Brotherhood of Evil Produce and keep the world safe from evil . . .

. . . but what do you do when evil shows up for your school *field trip*?!

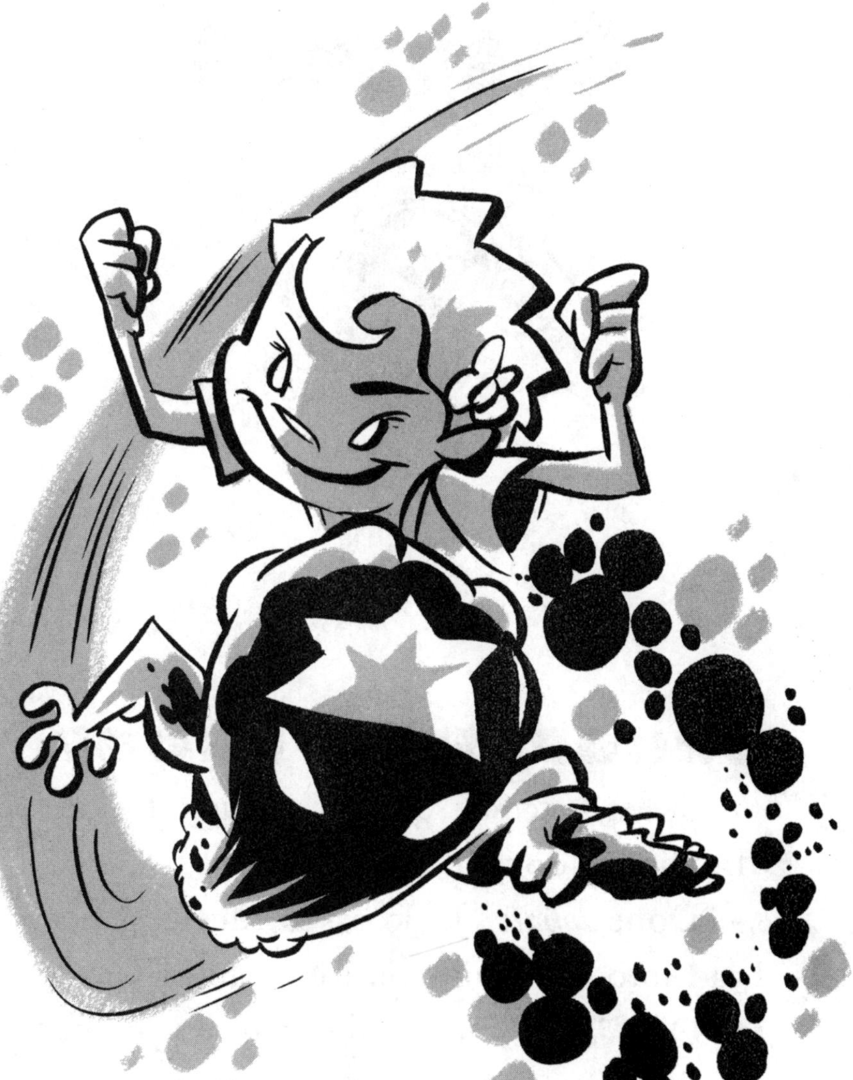

# Chapter 1

## BWOOPBWOOPBWOOP

"Sweet success!" cried the Magic Pickle. "I've finally done it!"

"Done *what*?" Jo Jo asked, ducking her head into the main control room of Capital Dill. "It's 7:30 in the morning—you shouldn't be doing anything! It's not like *you* need to get ready for school!"

"My specialized system of highly effective training techniques begins at dawn every morning," the Magic Pickle replied. "After push-ups, pull-ups, float-ups, a vinegar rinse, and organic dill renewal face washing, I begin my scenario exercises."

"Your *what*?!" Jo Jo laughed. She pulled up a chair and started brushing her hair. "It looks to me like you're playing a video game!"

# BWOOPBWOOPBWOOP
## ***GZLEEP!***

A computer-generated character appeared on the huge video monitor. It was a nose, a giant nose that glowed green around the nostrils. It dripped a digital drip of yuckiness splat in front of another character that looked like a big handkerchief, melting a big digital hole in its path.

"You may call it a game," sneered the Magic Pickle, "but mind exercise is essential in honing my crime-fighting abilities. Hand-eye coordination must be kept in tip-top shape if I'm to rid the world of the rancid indigestibles I so often cross paths with."

"So are you the nose or the handkerchief?" asked Jo Jo.

"I'll have you know that it's taken me hours to hack into this training program and assume the guise of the **Nostrillain**," said

the Magic Pickle. He pressed more buttons. "Your brother, Jason, is playing the **Handker Chief**, and he's unaware that I'm playing the Nostrillain. I'm certain your brother assumes he's battling the computer."

"Jason!" Jo Jo's eyes went wide. "NO!"

"Is there a problem?" asked the Magic Pickle. "Your brother is an inferior player,

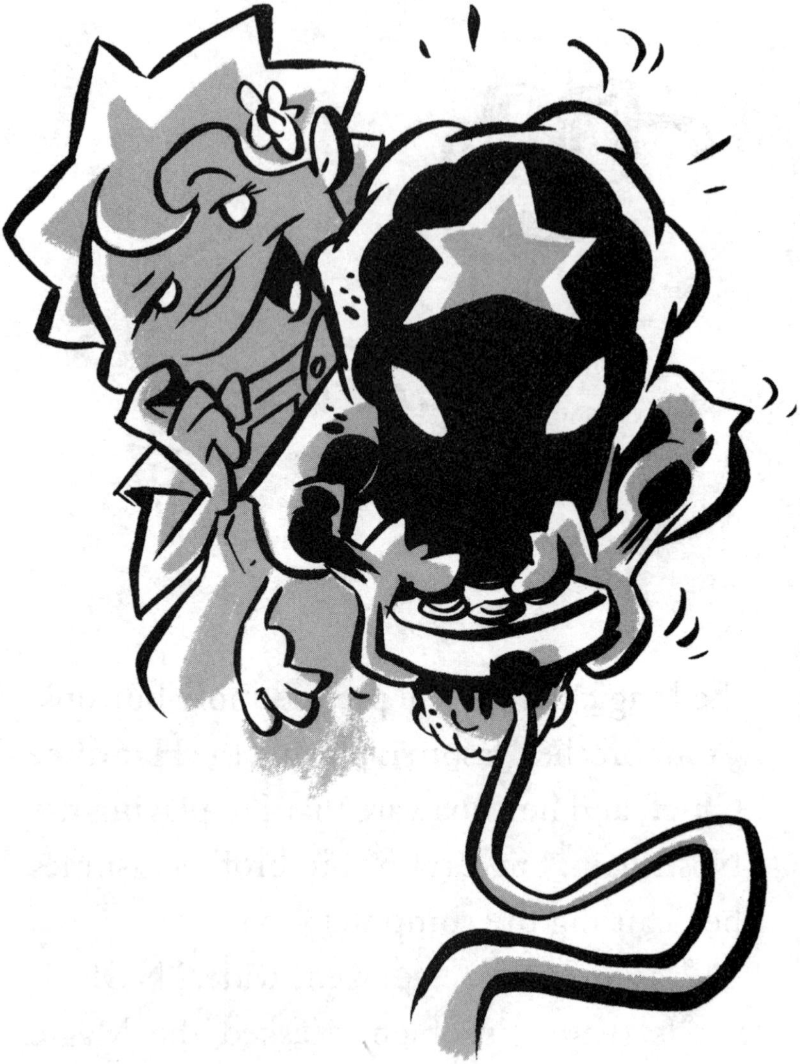

I assure you. There's no way he can defeat me."

"If Jason's playing video games," said Jo Jo, "that means he's in front of the television and therefore not ready to walk with me to the school bus stop. And I just *can't* miss the bus, not today!"

"And why is that?" asked the super-powered pickle.

"We're going on a school field trip to the peanut butter factory!" Jo Jo replied. She sped up the steps out of Capital Dill, dashed into her bedroom, and started frantically searching for her schoolbooks and backpack.

"Where *is* everything?" Jo Jo cried. She grabbed her backpack, threw it over her shoulder, and began tossing books and homework into it.

"Where's my notebook? I gotta have that notebook for my field trip!"

The Magic Pickle zipped into the room to help.

"Jo Jo, I—"

**WHACK!**

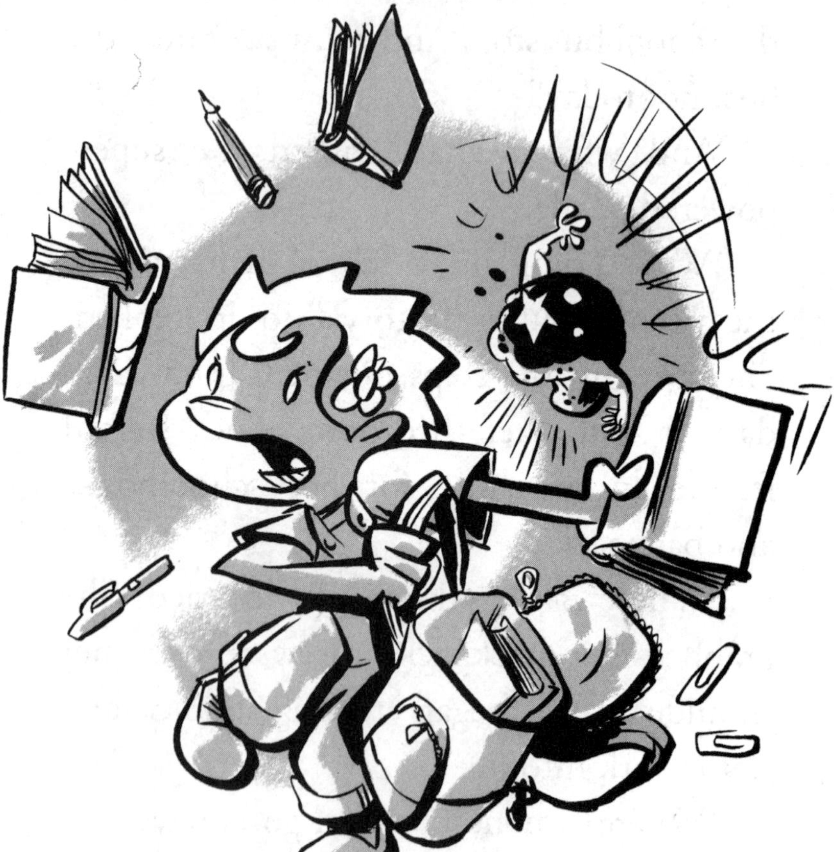

A thick math book bonked the Magic Pickle on the head and knocked him right into Jo Jo's backpack.

**ZIPPPPPPPPPPP!**

Without a glance, Jo Jo zipped up her backpack and stormed out of her room.

"JASON! You better be ready to move it!"

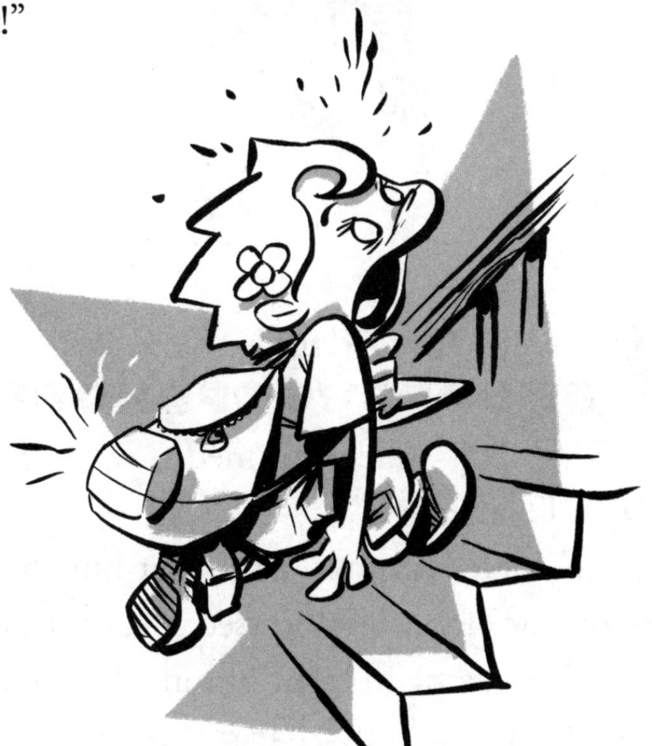

# Chapter 2

Jo Jo ran into the family room.

**BWOOPBWOOPBWOOP**

"JASON!!!" she screamed. "Will you MOVE IT already?!"

Jo Jo's older brother, Jason, sat hunched over on the floor, legs crossed, eyes staring at the video game in front of him. The only thing on Jason's body that moved were his thumbs. They rapidly pressed buttons on his game controller.

"Huh?" Jason replied. He was completely useless in the morning. Add in the fact that he was playing **SCHNOZOLA!** his favorite game, and you really had Jason at his worst. The boy could only concentrate on one thing at a time—and right now that one thing was SCHNOZOLA!

"C'mon!" Jo Jo whined. "We're going to miss the bus and I've got a school field trip today!!"

**BWOOPBWOOPBWOOP**

"Whuh?" Jason droned. He pressed a button and a game character ran circles around a small cat and then sneezed. "Ahuhuh!" Jason laughed. "Allergy attack."

"Come on!" Jo Jo insisted.

Jason gave Jo Jo the kind of "big brother" look that meant there was no way she was ever going to get what she wanted.

"Gimme a minute," Jason grunted. "I just started to win somehow. It's like the video game got dumb or something, or I got real good real quick!"

Jo Jo looked down and spotted her missing notebook spread wide open just under Jason's foot. A big, uncapped marker lay next to it. Jason's horrible handwriting was scribbled all over its pages.

"*WHAT ARE YOU DOING?!*" Jo Jo demanded. "You're *writing* in my *notebook*?!"

"What?" asked Jason, without looking up from the screen. "I'm making notes for secret moves and stuff. It's the only way I can beat the Nostrillain."

"*MOM!*" yelled Jo Jo. "Jason won't stop playing and take me to the bus. We're late, and he's ruining my notebook, and . . . !"

"Both of you better hustle out the door!" Mom replied. "You've got about two minutes before the bus arrives!"

"GAHHH!" Jo Jo squealed; she dashed out the door, backpack flapping behind her.

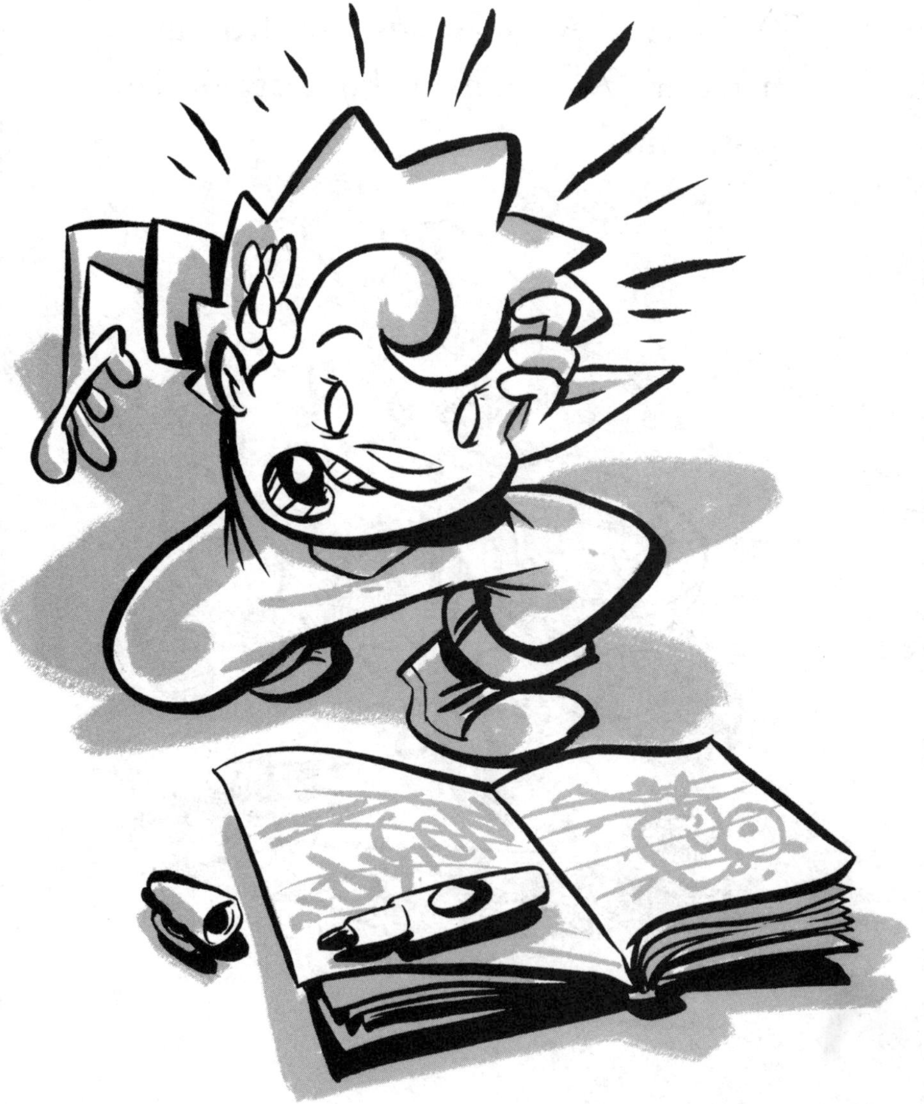

"Heh-heh," Jason chuckled at the TV screen. A large nose sniffed up his character. "Awww, man. I'll beat you later, Nostrillain."

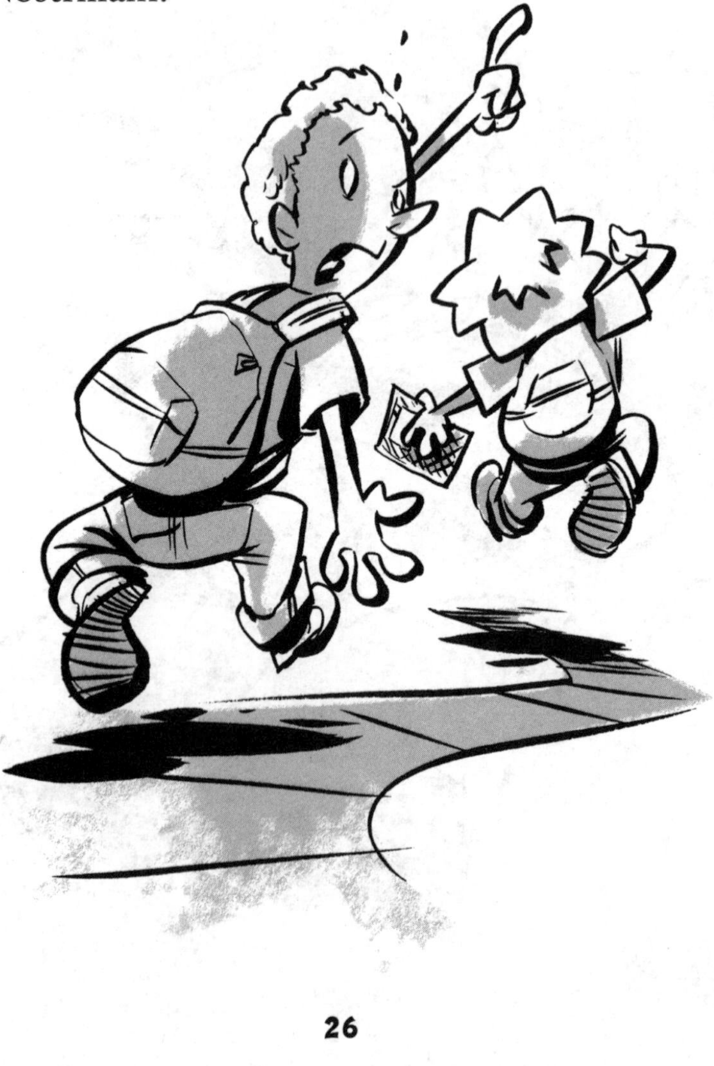

# Chapter 3

**J**o Jo pulled herself into the second bus seat she'd been in that morning. Luckily, she and Jason had caught the school bus (barely!) and got to school on time. Now Jo Jo's class was piling into the school bus again. Field trip time! Destination?

PETE'S PERFECT PEANUTS factory.

Miss Emilyek's class was going to find

out how peanuts were turned into peanut butter, peanut oil, and peanut-filled candy bars. Rumor had it that the factory gave out free samples to students on field trips. Jo Jo couldn't wait.

Jo Jo was sitting all the way in the back of the bus. She glanced at Ellen Cranston, her best buddy, in the next seat over. Ellen was sitting with Mikey Spuchins, their goofy but very good friend. Mikey had somehow managed to sneak his THINGAMADOO portable video game player onto the bus. Jo Jo looked to see what Mikey was playing.

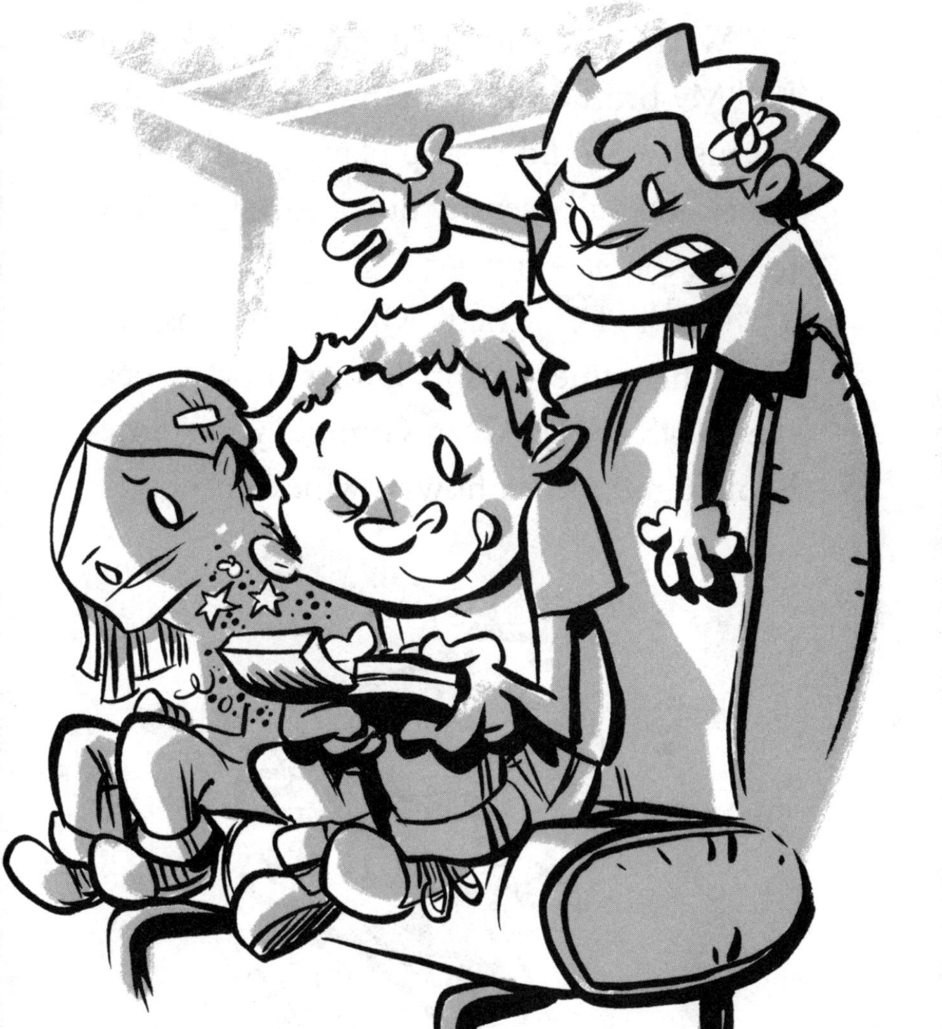

SCHNOZOLA!

"What *is it* with that game?!" asked Jo Jo. "My brother, Jason, almost made us late because he wouldn't stop playing it. Then he wrote notes all over my notebook about how to beat the bad guy—"

"WHUH?!" cried Mikey, looking up from the game. "Jason knows how to beat the NOSTRILLAIN? Gimme your notebook! I gotta learn how to wipe that nose!"

"No way." Jo Jo frowned. "And you better hide that thing before Miss Emilyek finds it and takes it away for good!"

"Yeah, Mikey," said Ellen. She grabbed the THINGAMADOO and tossed it into Mikey's backpack. "Concentrate on free candy bars. That's what today's about!"

Mikey perked up.

"Candy bars!" he said. "Free peanut-buttery, chocolate-covered candy bars . . ."

Ellen patted him on the back and turned to wink at Jo Jo. But Jo Jo was staring at the empty seat at the back of the bus. She leaned into the aisle for a closer look. A shriveled, blackened shell lodged in the crack of the bus seat.

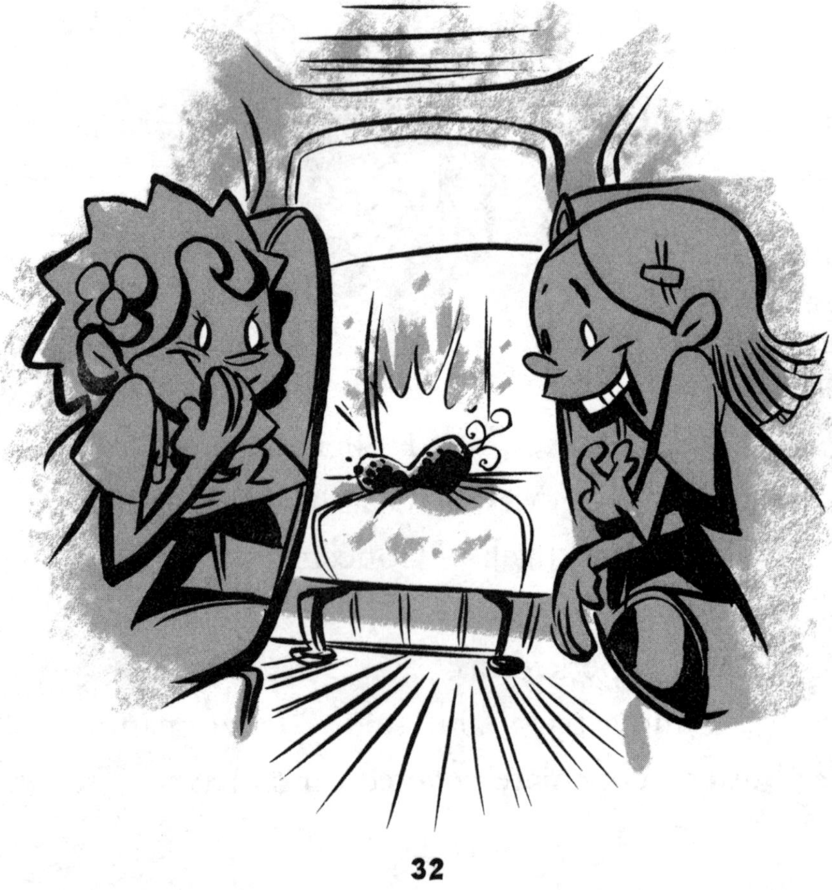

"What in the world is that thing?" she asked.

It looked like a twisted, rotten peanut.

"Maybe it's a stowaway!" Ellen replied. "You know, hitching a ride to the peanut factory to find his family!"

Both girls turned back around in their seats. Jo Jo couldn't help sneaking another peek, though. She had some unique firsthand experience with foods gone bad, but . . . Jo Jo shrugged. Seriously, it was highly unlikely that a small, funky old rotten peanut could do any damage. Besides, the bus was pulling up into the parking lot of PETE'S PERFECT PEANUTS.

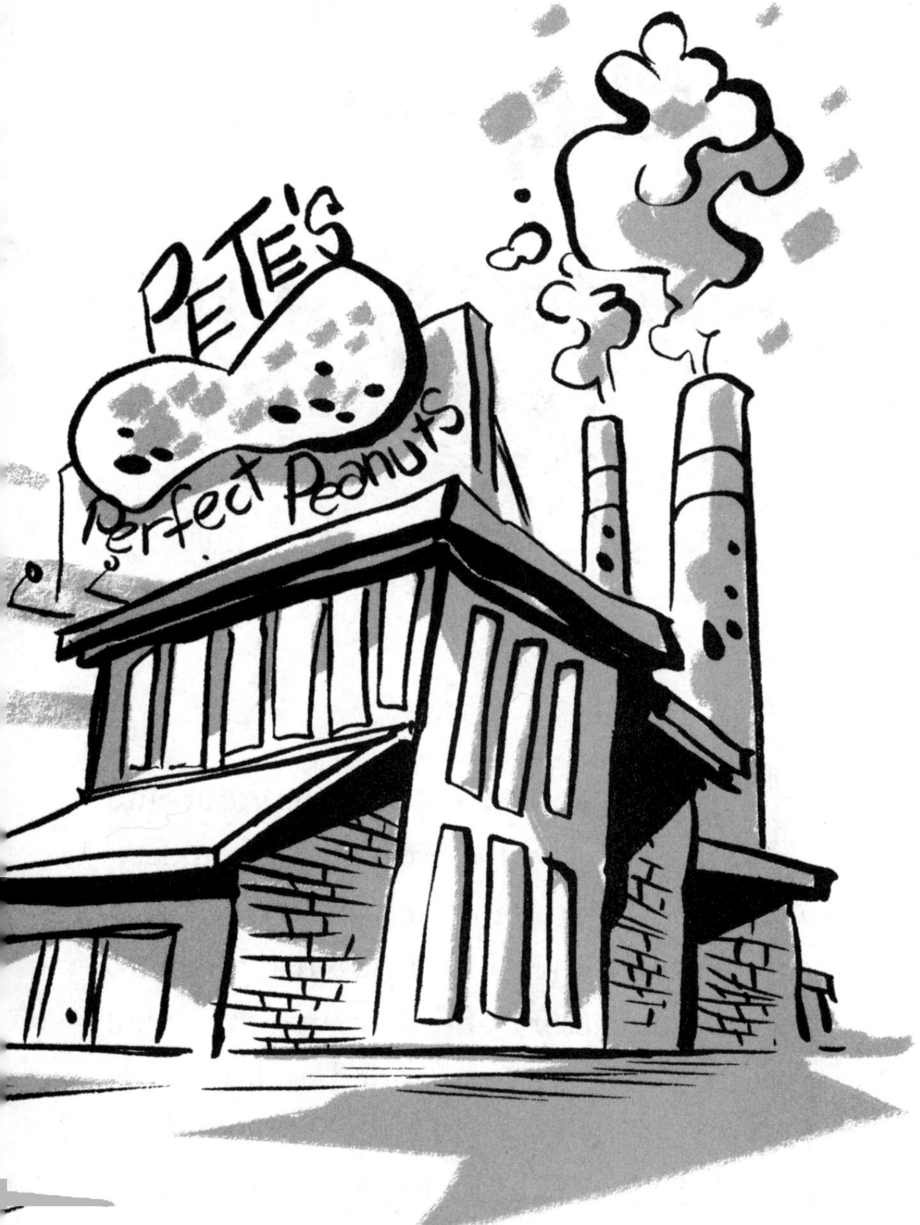
PETE'S
Perfect Peanuts

# Chapter 4

"**E**veryone, please stay in your group and be careful with these handheld guides," Miss Emilyek announced to the class.

Jo Jo and the rest of her class had filed into the peanut factory and split up into small groups. Their teacher handed each group a PETE'S PERFECT PEANUTS handheld digital guide. With the press of a button on

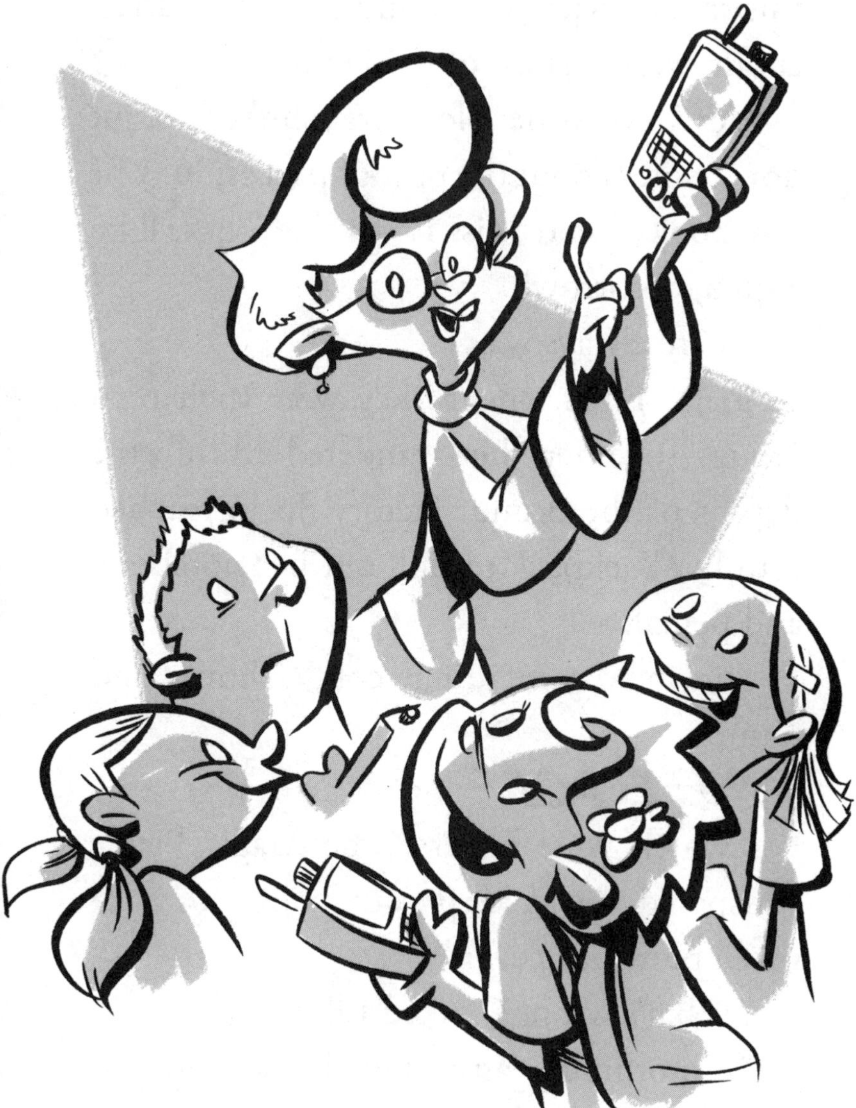

this small device, you could get information about every section of the factory.

"And everyone please remember to jot down notes about the peanut process in your notebooks," said Miss Emilyek. "There'll be a quiz tomorrow!"

There always was.

Jo Jo, Ellen, and Mikey were their own group. Together, they wandered off into the depths of the peanut factory. Jo Jo reached into her backpack to pull out her notebook and pencil.

She felt something cold, slimy, and bumpy.

**"EEK!"**

"Watch your fingers," the Magic Pickle whispered. "And keep your voice down or you'll blow our cover!"

"What's wrong?" asked Ellen.

"N-nothing," answered Jo Jo. "I just poked my finger with my pencil."

# BOOP!

Mikey pressed a button and the PETE'S
PERFECT PEANUTS guide displayed
and read aloud information about the
peanut sorting conveyor belt they were
standing near. Ellen and Mikey listened
and took notes; Jo Jo peeked back inside
her backpack.

"What are you doing here?" Jo Jo hissed.

"You waylaid me with a math book and I was brought along for your field trip against my will," the Magic Pickle replied. "I assure you, my time would be much better spent back at headquarters honing my battle skills with a game of SCHNOZOLA!"

"Just stay quiet and we'll be home before you know it," Jo Jo whispered back. "Plus, if you play your cards right, you might end up sitting next to a free candy bar!"

"Jo Jo, look!" called Ellen. "Doesn't that look like that gross old peanut from the bus?"

Ellen pointed up at the conveyor belt overhead, which rattled along carrying peanut after peanut through the factory. Sure enough, a blackened, twisted, rotten-looking peanut rolled along on the belt.

It *was* the same peanut from the bus.

"I wonder how that thing got here?" said Jo Jo. She stared at the weird-looking peanut . . . which had stopped moving!

Suddenly the peanut shell began to flicker like a lightbulb. A creepy, black lightbulb.

**FWWAARRRZZZZAAAAKKKKK!!!**

The gnarly peanut exploded, the two halves of its shell falling to the ground.

**"BWAHAHAHAHAH!!!"**

cried a villainous voice. "Behold the **Black Legume**! Prepare to fall to your knees under a gooey cover of doom! With my spread of peanut-buttery evil, you'll all be immobilized, and then *I* will take over as supreme leader of

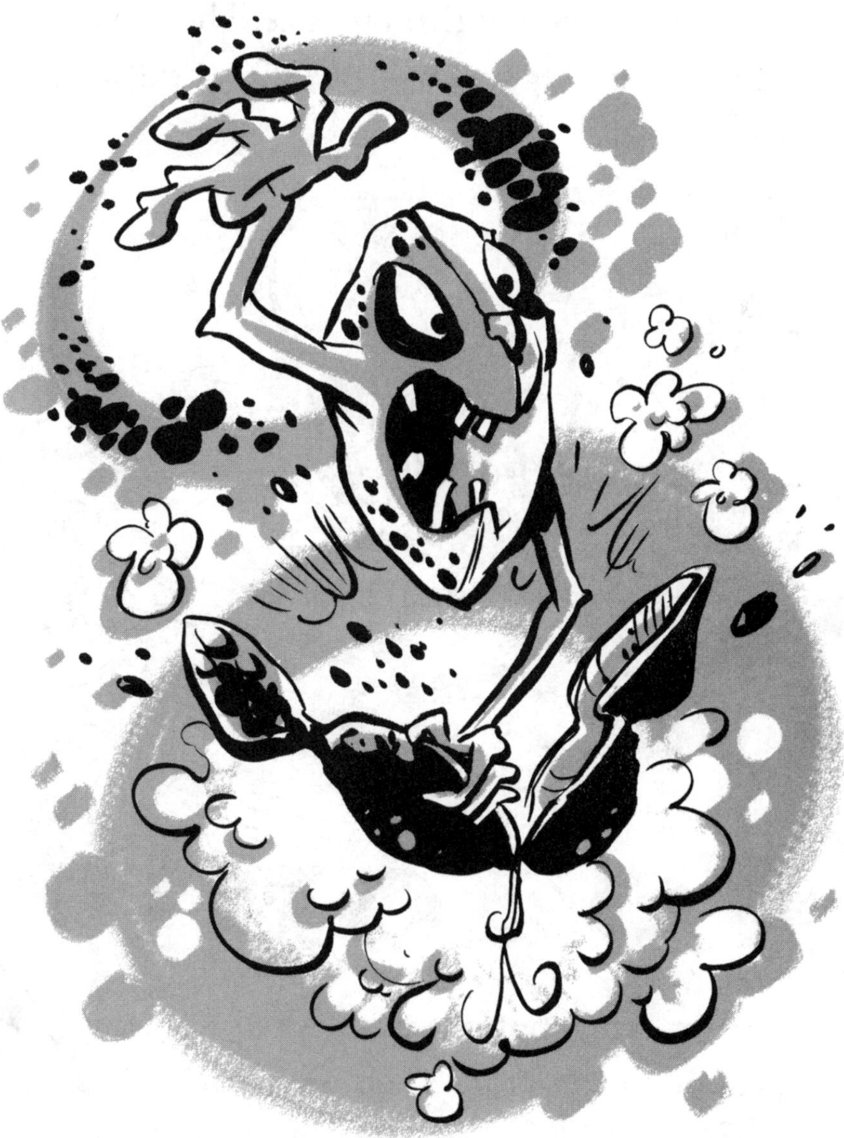

the Brotherhood of Evil Produce! The power of the Black Legume will rule the world!"

FOOOM!!!

Two arms shot out of the shell, spraying peanut butter from their fingertips. In a second, Ellen and Mikey were completely covered in peanut butter and couldn't see or move.

A flash of green burst from Jo Jo's backpack and pushed her under the conveyor belt.

"Take cover!" the Magic Pickle shouted.

"That thing is NUTS!" cried Jo Jo.

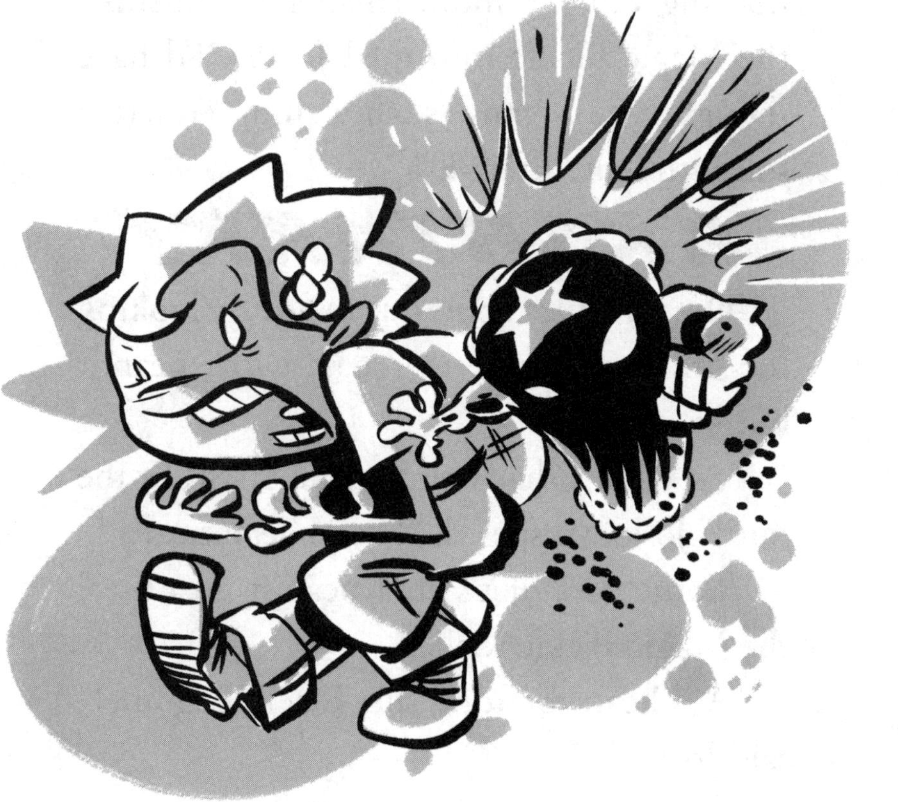

"It isn't nuts, technically," the Magic Pickle said.

"WHAT?!" Jo Jo exclaimed. "If that thing isn't nuts, then what is it?"

"A legume. A peanut is a legume, an organism formed from two identical halves, housing one or more smaller organisms," the Magic Pickle informed Jo Jo. "I'd have thought you'd know such a thing. You're a solid student, after all."

**KKSHTAKK!**

The Creature spun out in a fury, looking for more victims to coat with peanut butter.

"So who is that weirdo from INSIDE the nut?!" Jo Jo whispered. "I mean legume. . . ."

"Some sort of twisted peanut creature," the Magic Pickle replied.

"A Creature from the Black Legume!" said Jo Jo.

# Chapter 5

Jo Jo and the Magic Pickle watched in horror as the Creature from the Black Legume zoomed around the factory, blasting Jo Jo's classmates with peanut butter.

"We've got to stop him!" said Jo Jo. She watched as her archenemy, Lu Lu Deederly, that science kid Jarek Sredanka, and the rest of their group, Isabel Tanner, Abbie Zorito,

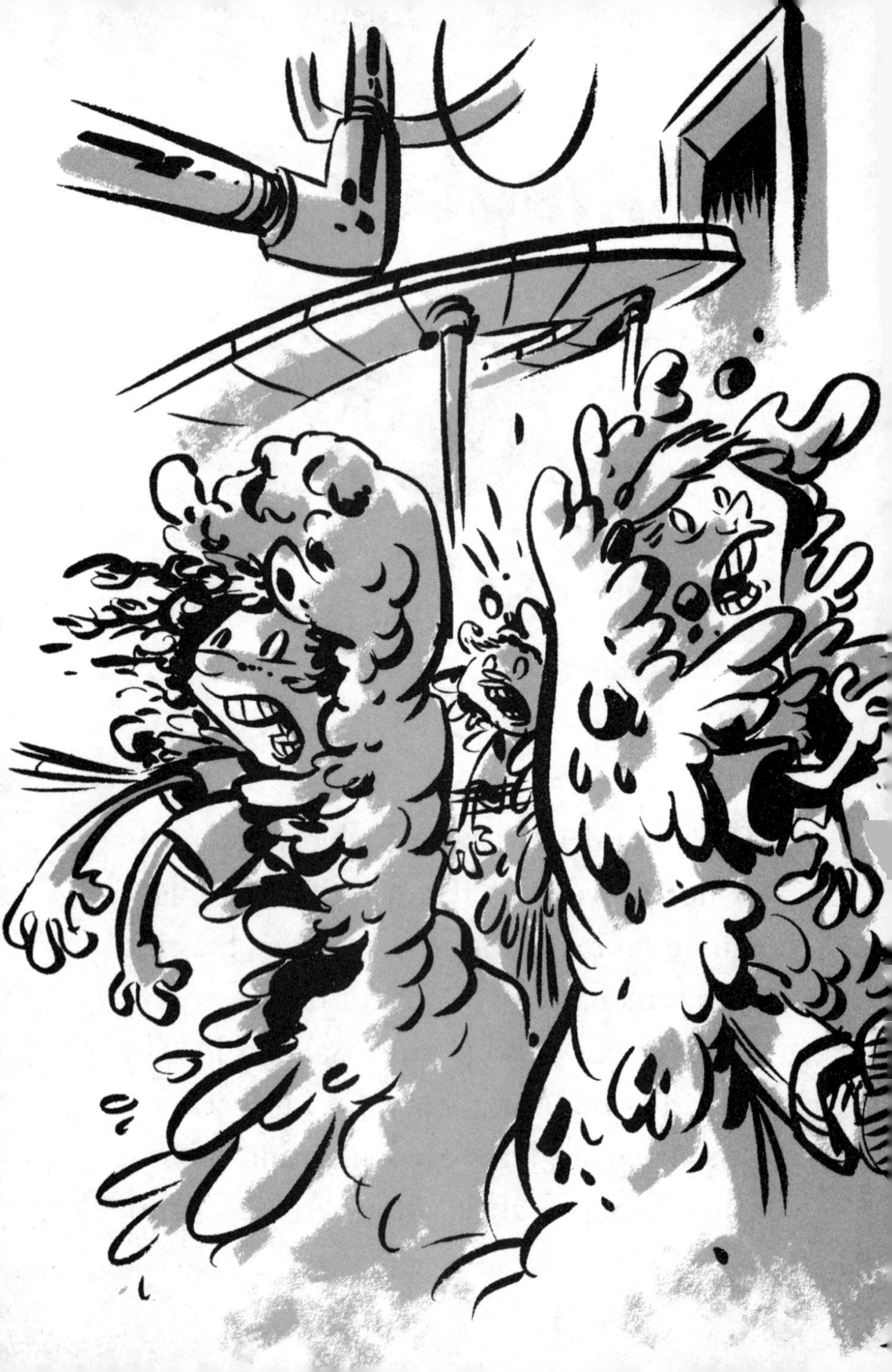

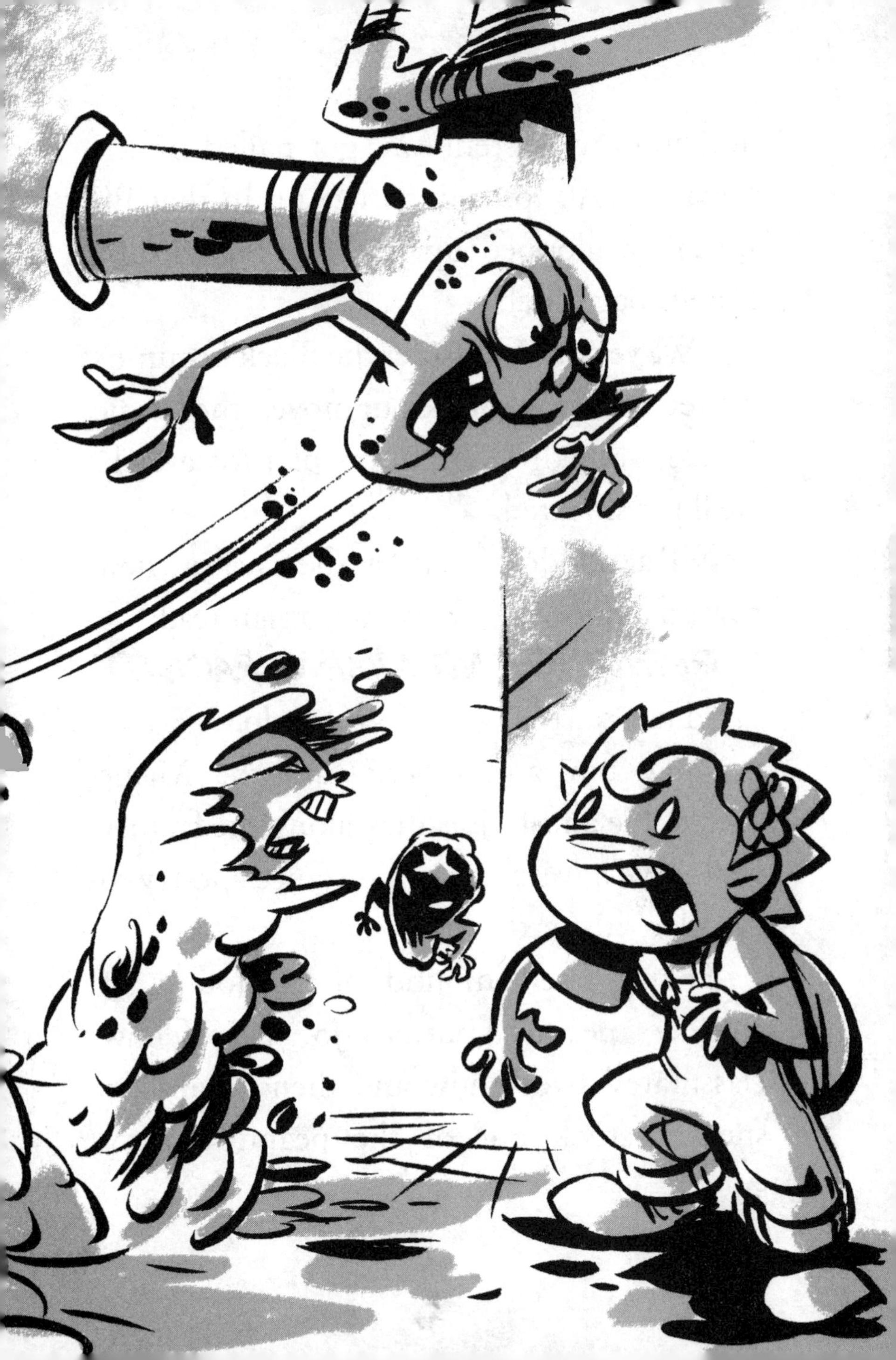

and Johnny Austenbean, got nailed by the Creature. All four kids froze up in that PB instantly, glopped up like one big, drippy brown-bag lunch.

"We've got to consider the Black Legume's powers before we make our move," the Magic Pickle warned. "Without a plan of attack, we'll get smeared."

MP and Jo Jo watched as the Creature flew toward a doorway. Overhead, a sign read:

**GRINDING AND MIXING FACILITY**

"That can't be good," said Jo Jo.

"Stay low and quiet," said the Magic Pickle. He and Jo Jo snuck along the factory wall. "We'll watch from a distance and try to calculate his next move."

They passed mound after mound of chunky peanut butter—Jo Jo's fellow classmates! Every now and then a hand or sneaker stuck out of the peanut-buttery goo.

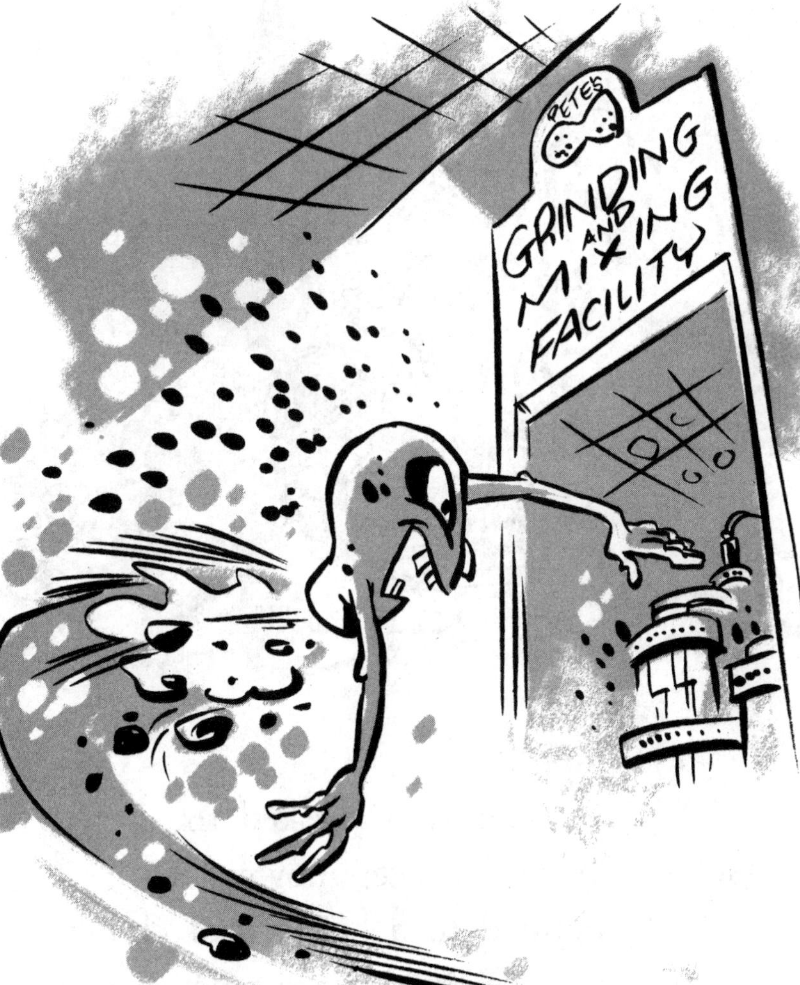
PETE'S
GRINDING AND MIXING FACILITY

Jo Jo stopped.

"What's the matter?" asked the Magic Pickle. "We need to keep moving."

Jo Jo pointed to a big pile of chunky peanut butter wearing horn-rimmed glasses, just like Miss Emilyek's.

"I think he gooed my teacher!" said Jo Jo.

"Steel your nerves, girl," said MP. "This is no time to turn to jelly! That villain's wretchedness will spread thin and we'll find his weak spot!"

"Oh, WILL you?!"

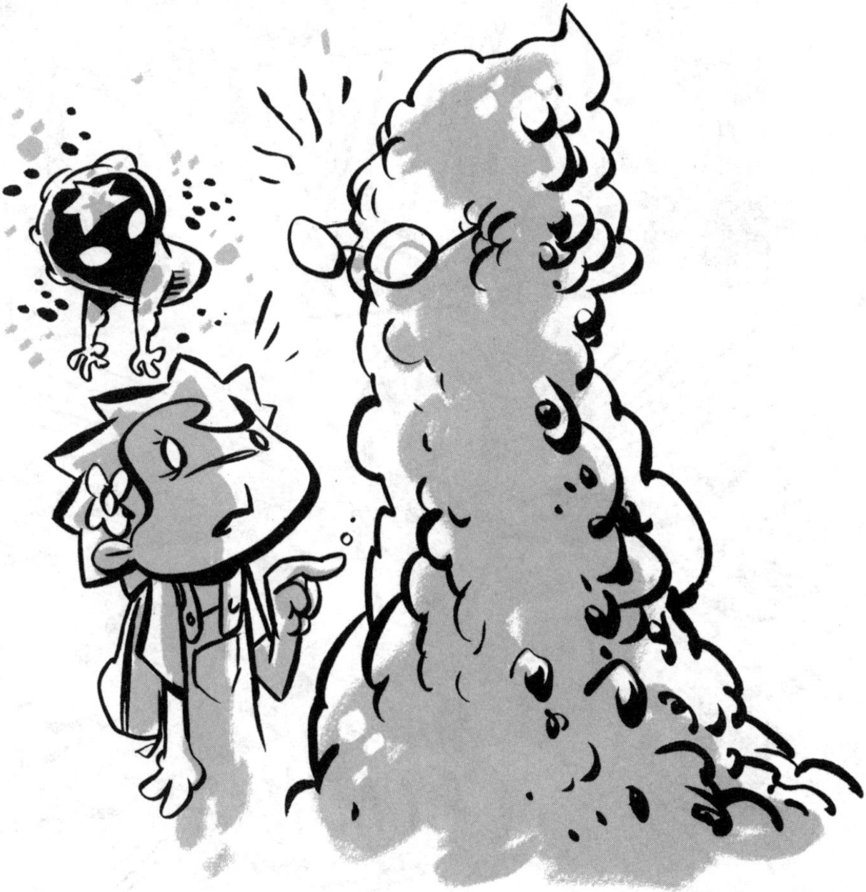

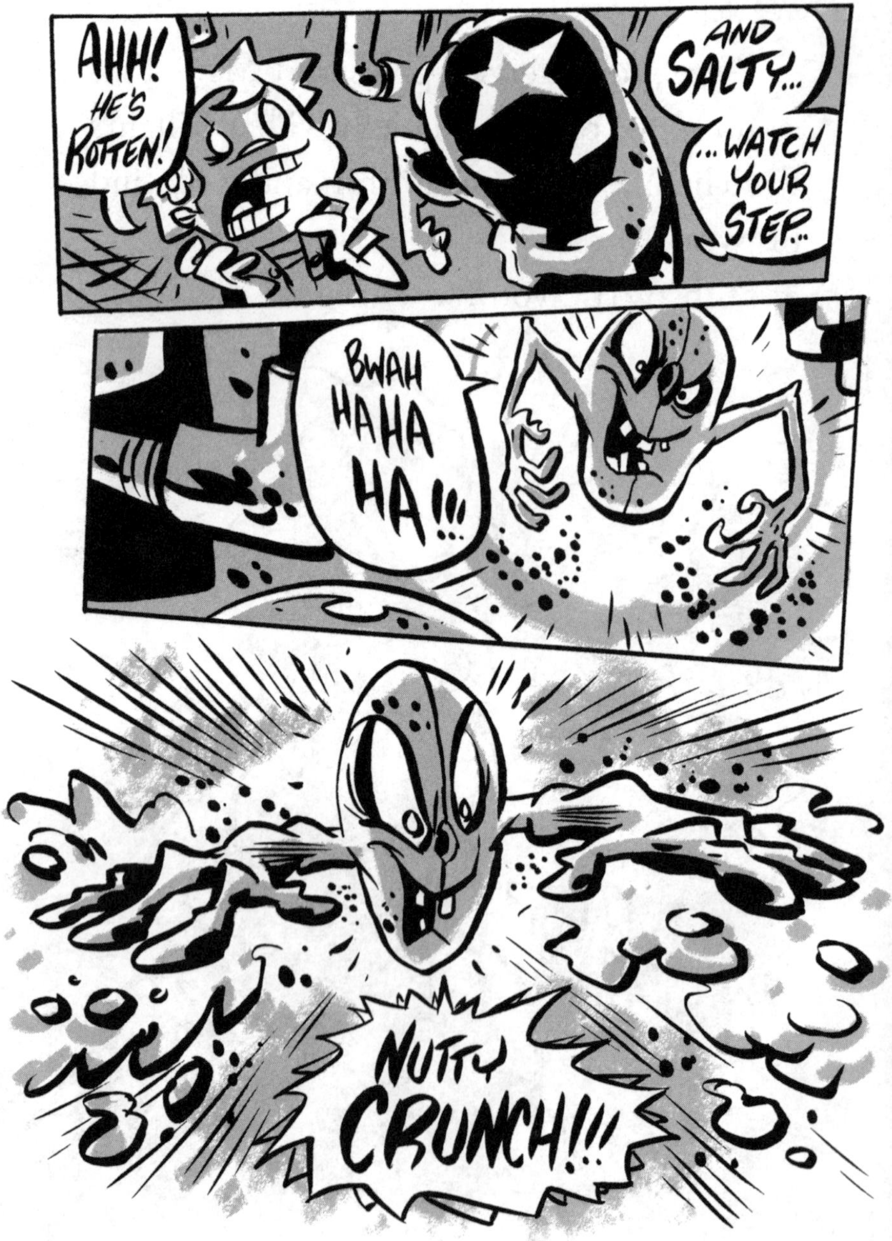
AHH! HE'S ROTTEN!
AND SALTY...
...WATCH YOUR STEP...
BWAH HAHAHA HA!!!
NUTTY CRUNCH!!!

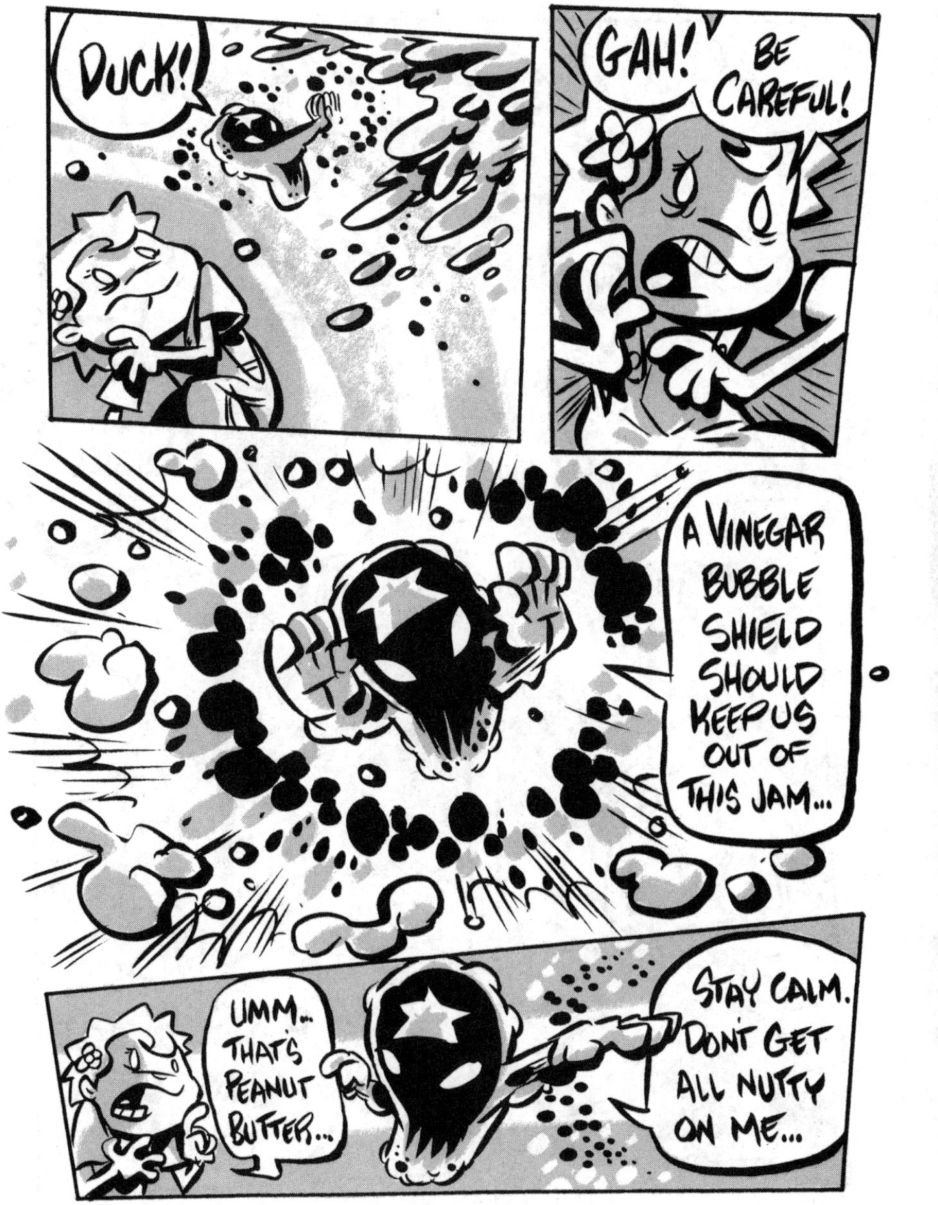
DUCK!
GAH!
BE CAREFUL!
A VINEGAR BUBBLE SHIELD SHOULD KEEP US OUT OF THIS JAM...
UMM... THAT'S PEANUT BUTTER...
STAY CALM. DON'T GET ALL NUTTY ON ME...

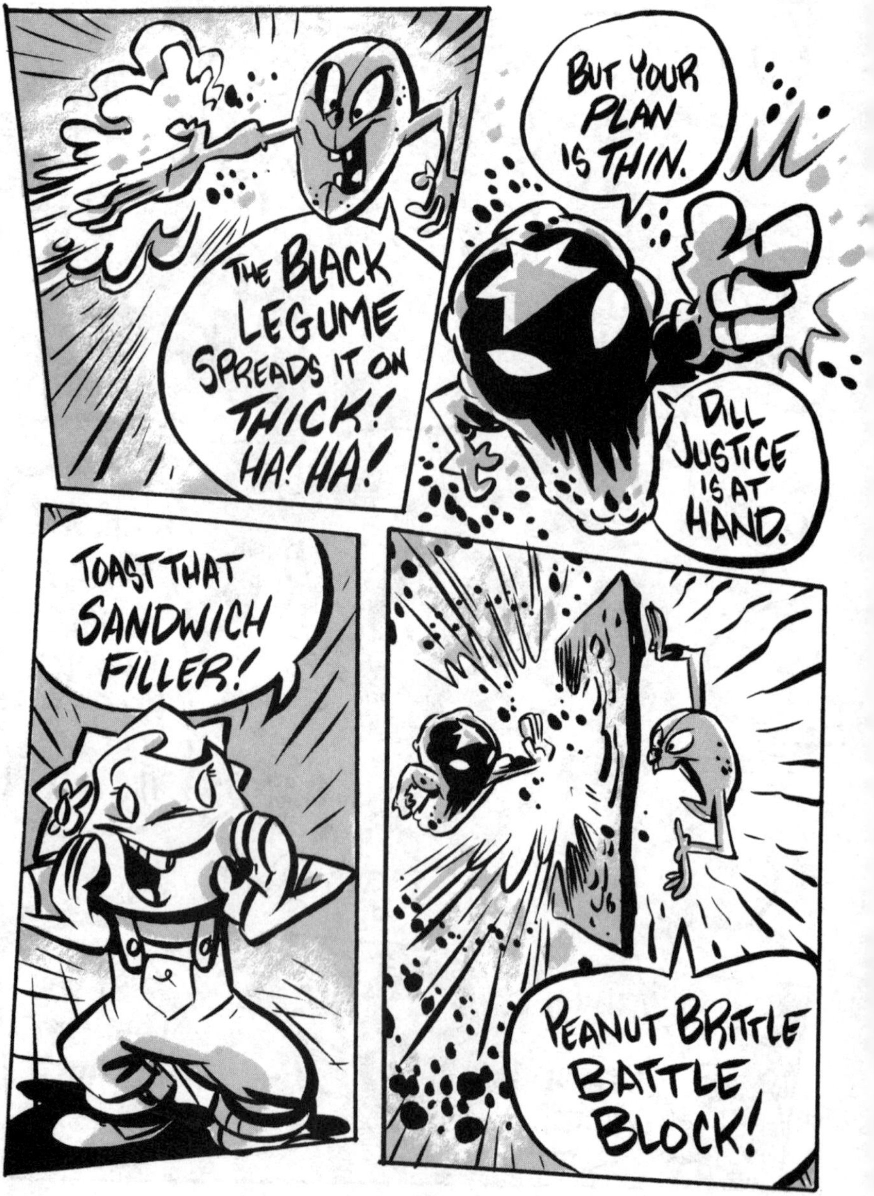
THE BLACK LEGUME SPREADS IT ON THICK! HA! HA!
BUT YOUR PLAN IS THIN.
DILL JUSTICE IS AT HAND.
TOAST THAT SANDWICH FILLER!
PEANUT BRITTLE BATTLE BLOCK!

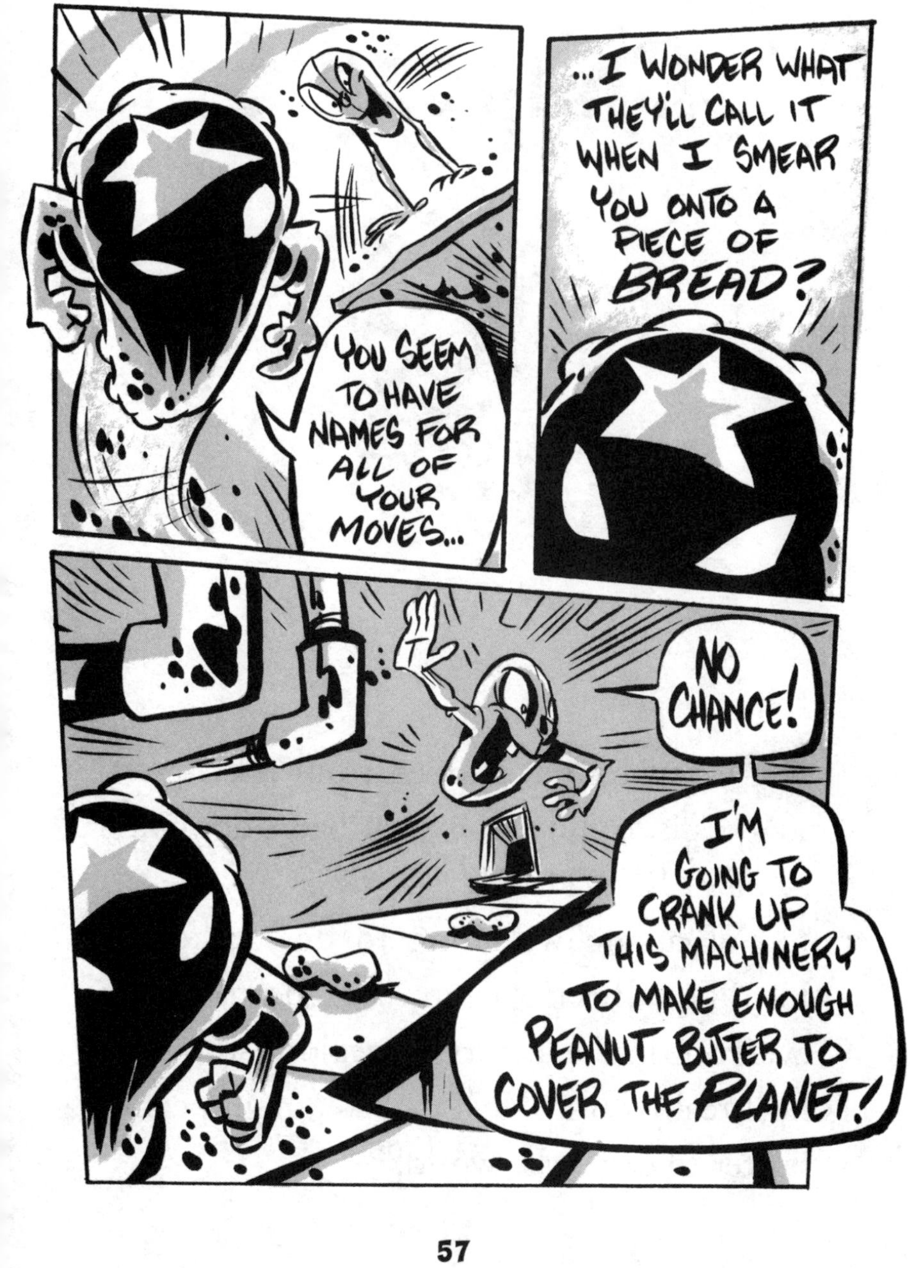
YOU SEEM TO HAVE NAMES FOR ALL OF YOUR MOVES...
...I WONDER WHAT THEY'LL CALL IT WHEN I SMEAR YOU ONTO A PIECE OF BREAD?
NO CHANCE!
I'M GOING TO CRANK UP THIS MACHINERY TO MAKE ENOUGH PEANUT BUTTER TO COVER THE PLANET!

# Chapter 6

**P**eanut butter dripped from the factory walls, ceiling, conveyor belts, doorways . . . EVERYWHERE!

"What are we going to do?" asked Jo Jo. "The Black Legume is gumming up everyone in the factory. If we don't stop him, he'll really do it! He'll make enough peanut butter to cover the world!"

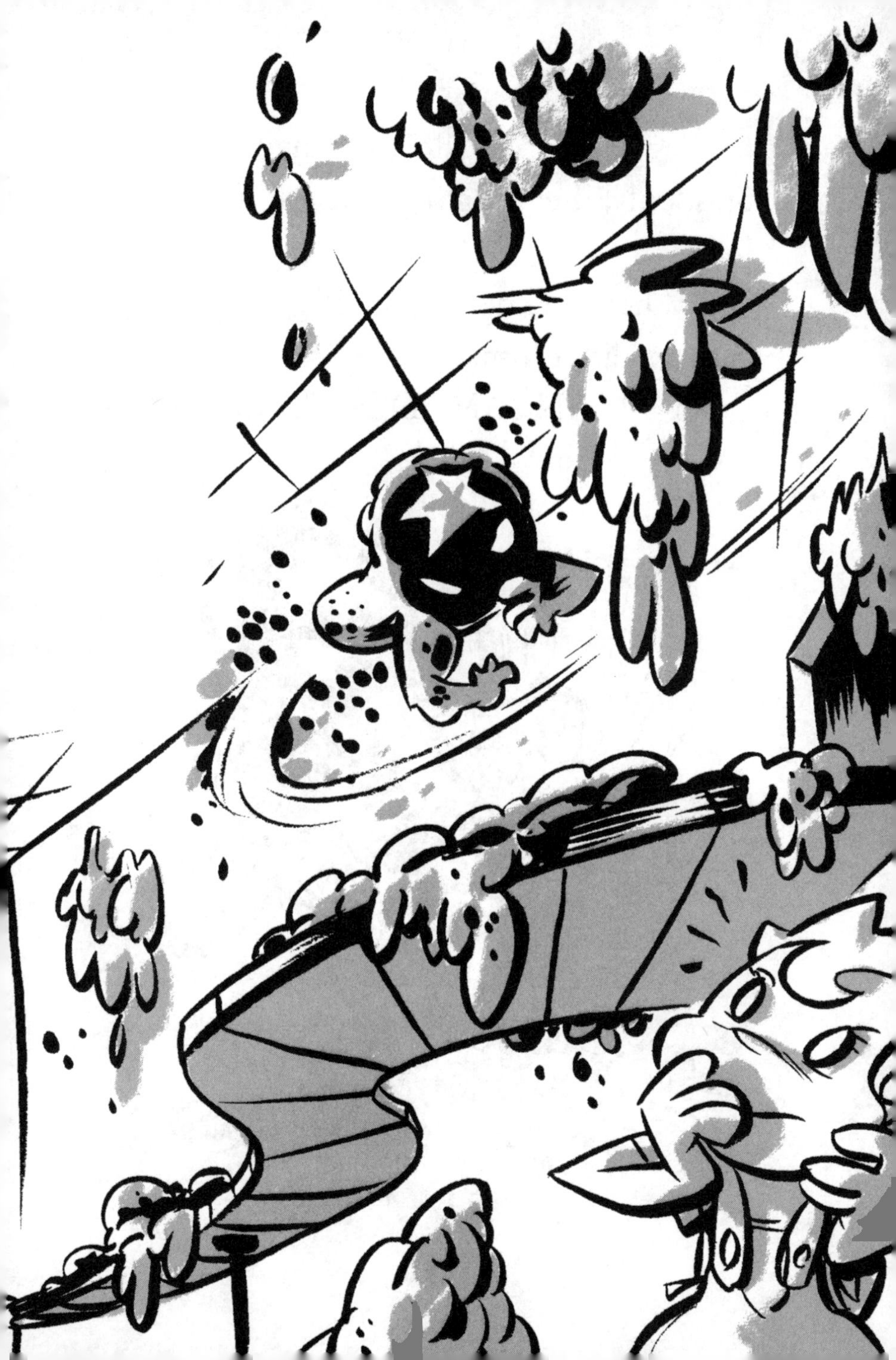

The Magic Pickle scratched his head. Suddenly, he caught sight of a blinking light.

"Where are you going?!" called Jo Jo, running after him.

"A THINGAMADOO!" the Magic

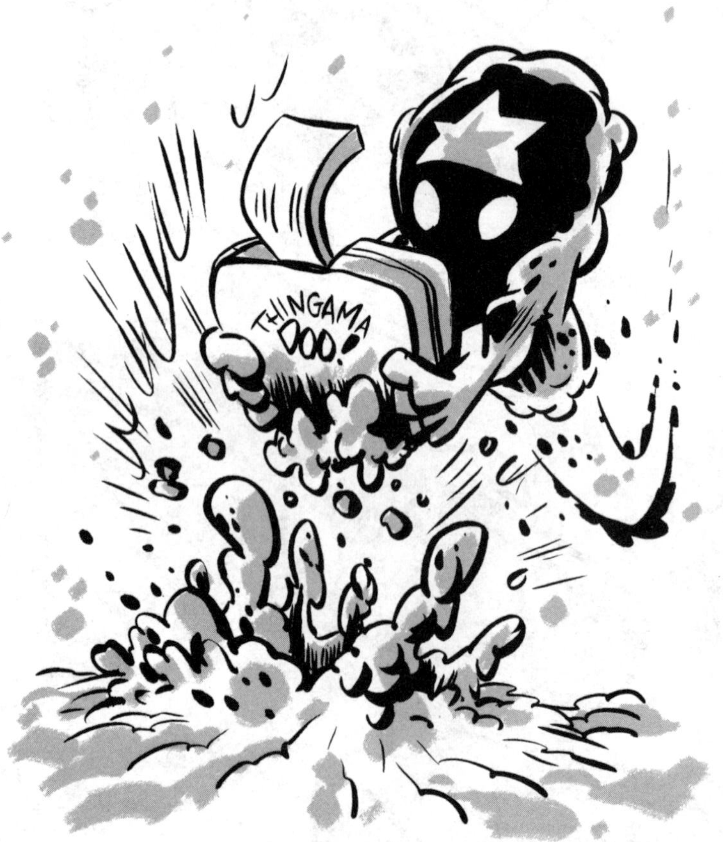
THINGAMA
DOO!

Pickle replied. He zoomed down and pulled the game player out of a sticky mound of peanut butter.

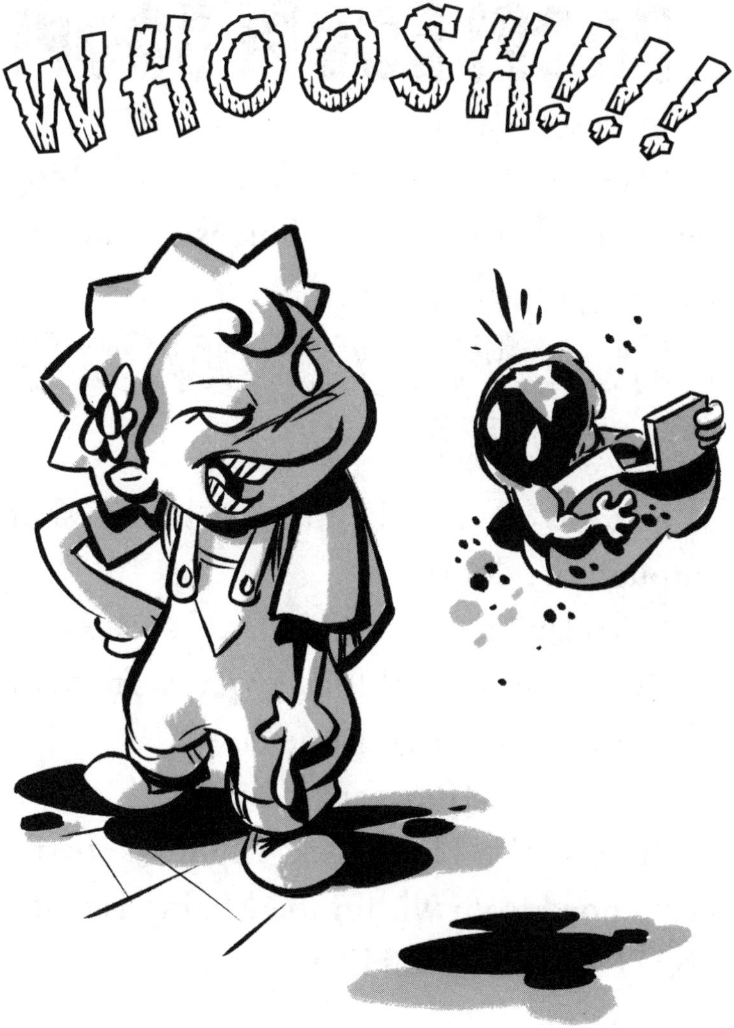
WHOOSH!!!

"That's Mikey's!" said Jo Jo. "And this must be Mikey." She stuck her finger into the mound of peanut butter.

# BOOP! BOOP! BOOP!

Jo Jo spun around.

"Are you seriously PLAYING that thing right now?!" she asked. "This is no time to be going for a high score!"

# SPLOOARRCH! SPLOOARRCH! SPLOOARRCH!

Streams of chunky peanut butter shot through the doorway.

"He's laying down cover fire!" shouted Jo Jo. "Or cover butter! Either way, we're toast if he hits us! Put that game down!"

"But I—" MP began.

"HA-HA!" The Black Legume's battle cry echoed from within the Mixing Facility. "NUTTY CRUNCH!"

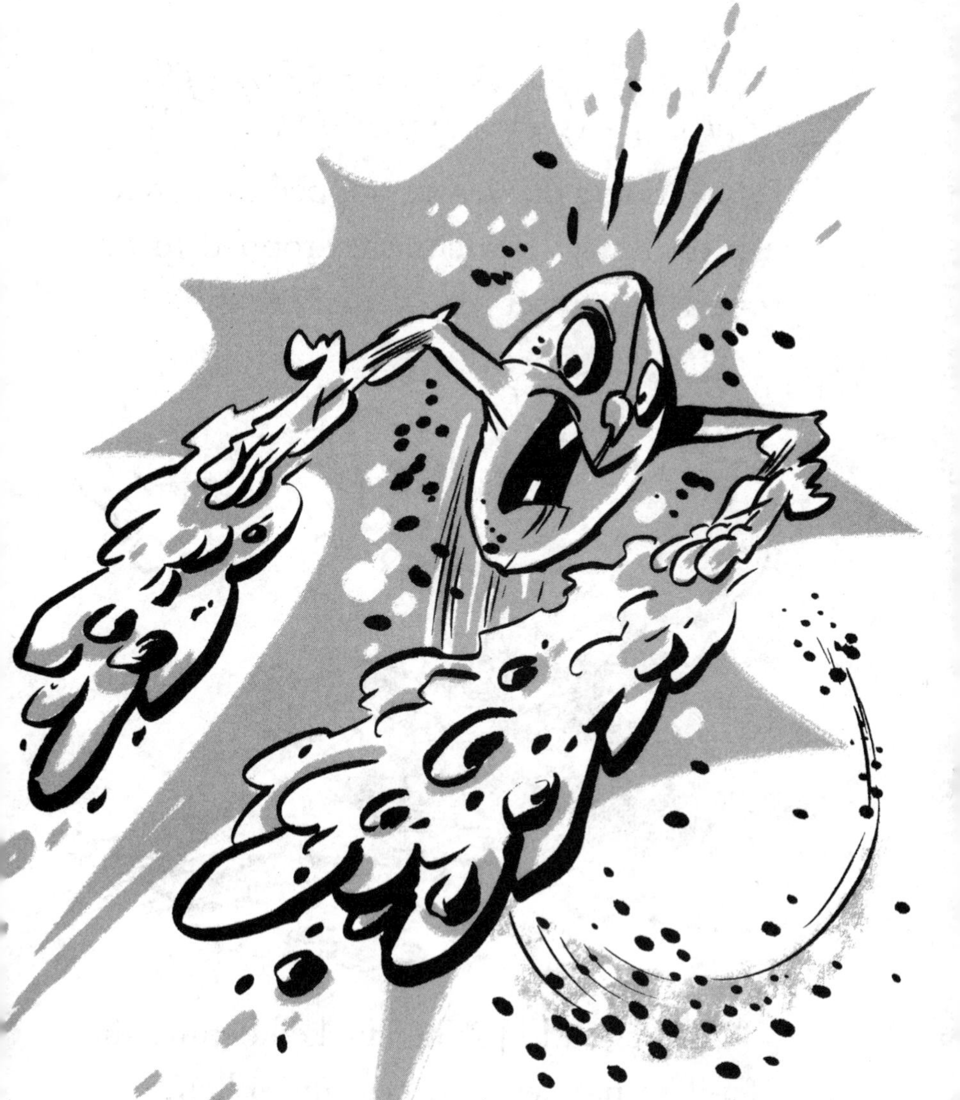

# SPLOOARRCH!

The Magic Pickle was trapped by a gooey heap of Nutty Crunch. He dropped to the ground with a wet

# SPLATT!

"No!" cried Jo Jo. She ducked behind the PB piles that were Mikey and Ellen. The Black Legume Creature peered out of the doorway and cackled.

"Peanut brains!" he shouted. "This world domination thing is going to be smooth as butter." He flew back into the Mixing Facility.

# KCHUNK! KCHUNK!

"Oh no," Jo Jo whimpered. "He's starting the machines! He's making more peanut butter!"

# Chapter 7

"Come on, get up!" said Jo Jo. The Magic Pickle tried to fly, but he was completely covered in sticky Nutty Crunch.

"Why'd you stop to play that lousy game, anyway?" she asked. "Your silly love of SCHNOZOLA! just got you smeared!"

"I was . . . hoping to find . . . an idea," said

MP. His voice was thick with peanut butter glob. "Some way to . . . defeat the . . . Creature . . ."

"I thought we were going to watch him and try to discover a weakness," Jo Jo said. "You should have stuck to the plan! Now you're just stuck to the floor!"

"Well," said the Magic Pickle, "in my

game training scenarios, there's often a clue that will help you ward off an attack. For example, the Nostrillain always announces his MO before striking, like 'NOSE GOBLIN!' or 'SNEEZE FREEZE!' The Black Legume also seems to announce his attack plans as well. Remember 'NUTTY CRUNCH' and 'PEANUT BRITTLE BATTLE BLOCK'? I thought I could find a game clue that might work here, too. If only I knew the game better."

"SCHNOZOLA! is not going to solve our problem!" said Jo Jo firmly. She started pacing, but then spotted a PETE'S PER-FECT PEANUTS guide on the floor. Her eyes grew wide. She grabbed the device and quickly pressed a button. A map of the fac-tory appeared; all the rooms in the place were labeled.

"Oh, now *you* can play games but *I* can't?" MP sneered.

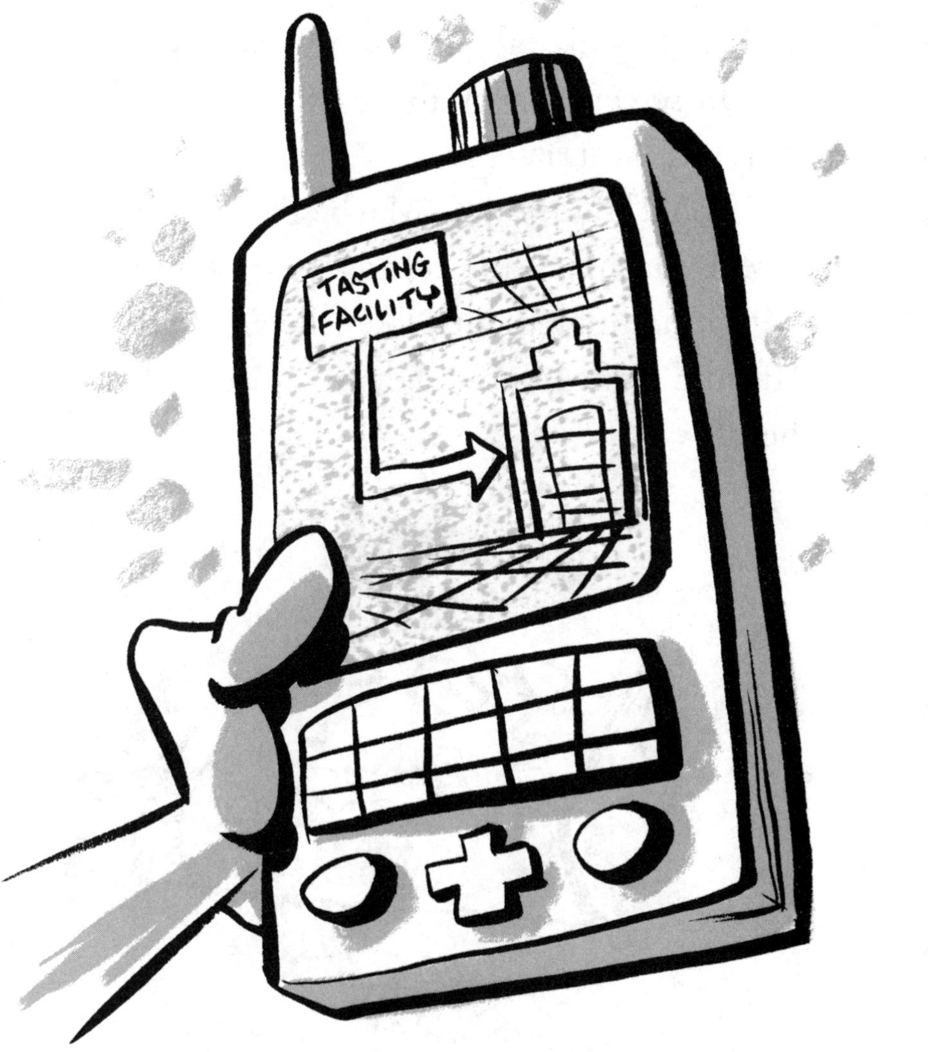
TASTING FACILITY

"This isn't a game, ya silly dilly," replied Jo Jo. "It's a digital guide to the factory."

On screen, a sign above one room read: TASTING FACILITY

"Look!" said Jo Jo. "Maybe Pete's has different machines for testing peanut butter with other ingredients, like jelly and chocolate and stuff! I know they make candy bars here."

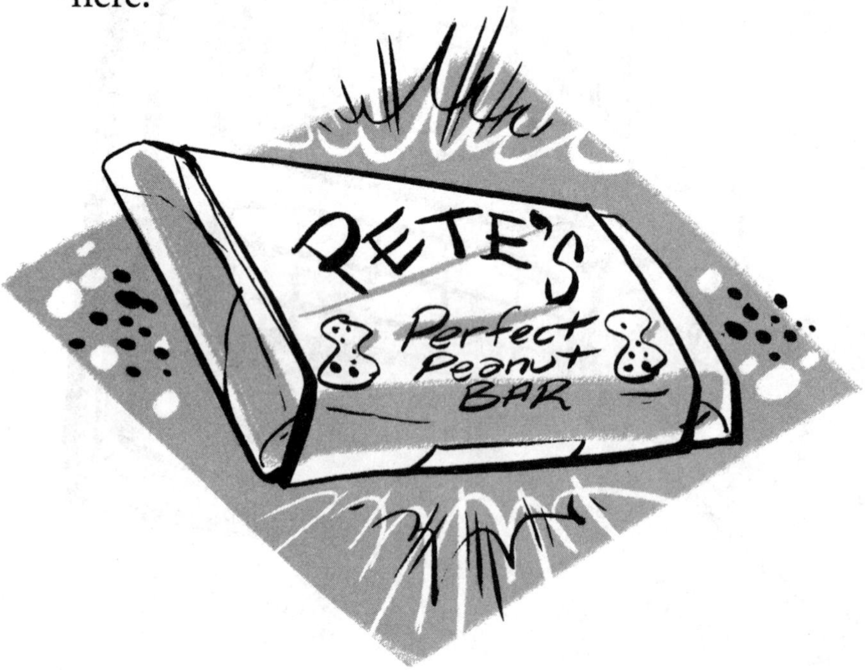
PETE'S
Perfect
Peanut
BAR

"I never indulge in sweets," said the Magic Pickle. "Hardly the way to keep your body in shape for crime fighting."

"Stay here. I'm going to look for something to fight that Creature with," said Jo Jo. She ran toward the Tasting Facility.

"I'll just stick around," said MP.

# Chapter 8

Jo Jo stumbled into the Tasting Facility. The room was full of people-shaped mounds of peanut butter. The short ones were her fellow classmates, the taller ones the factory workers.

She looked around and saw huge vats hanging from the ceiling. Tubes pumped chocolate and caramel and nougat from vat to vat.

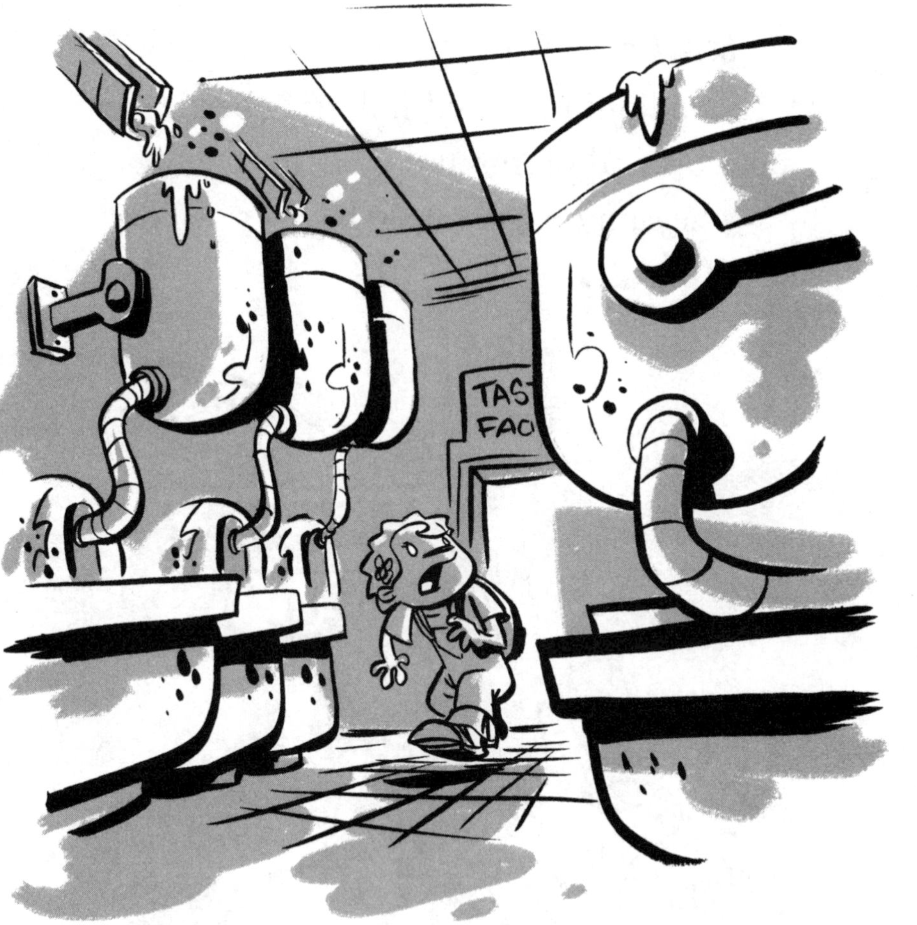
TAST
FAC

"There!" said Jo Jo. "THAT one might work!"

Jo Jo climbed up to a vat filled with thick, swirling red liquid.

**SNIFFF!!!**

The liquid smelled like strawberries and apricots and plums and grapes.

The sign on the vat said:

*JELLY*

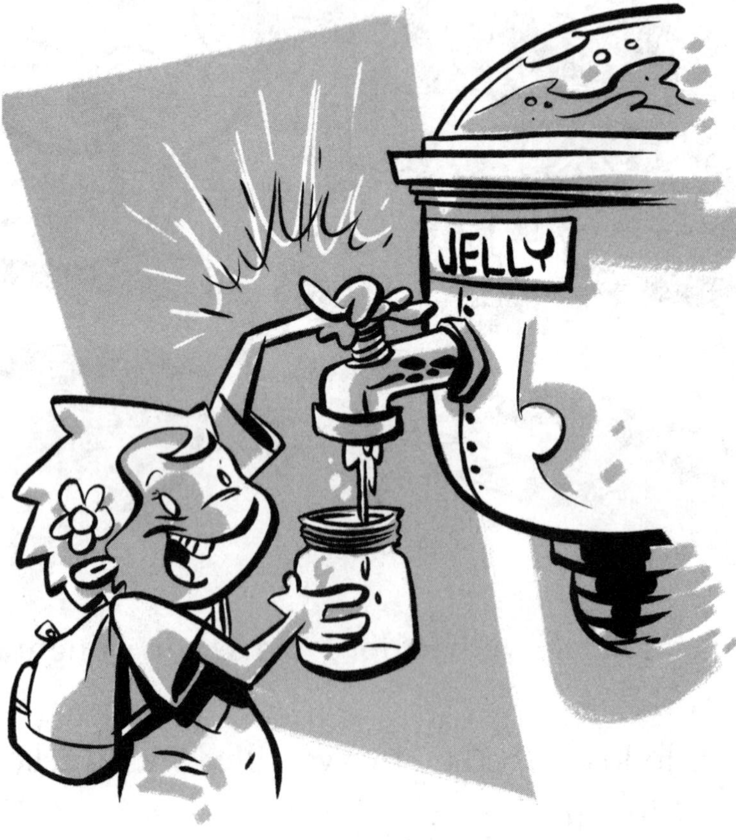
JELLY

"Let's see how the Black Legume does when he's smeared with this!" Jo Jo said. She grabbed some empty jars, turned on the jelly tube, and filled the jars with the thick red liquid. Then she screwed on the lids and raced back to the Magic Pickle.

"What have you got? A secret weapon?" asked MP. "Spill the beans!"

"You mean spill the JELLY!" Jo Jo answered.

She poured a full jar of jelly over the mound of peanut butter that covered the Magic Pickle. The peanut butter began to soften and smear together with the jelly. MP struggled inside the gooey glop.

# SPLOOCH!

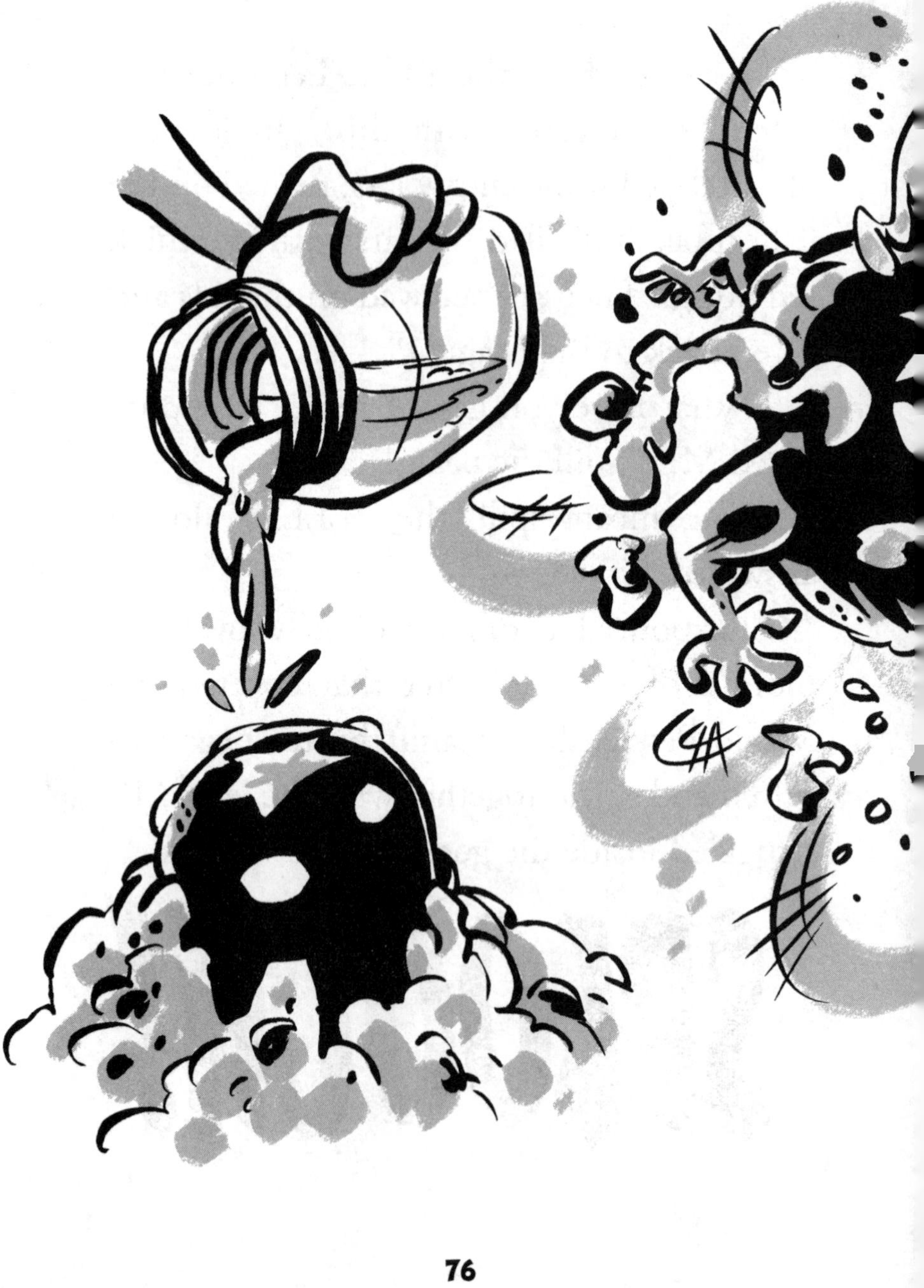
CHA
CHA

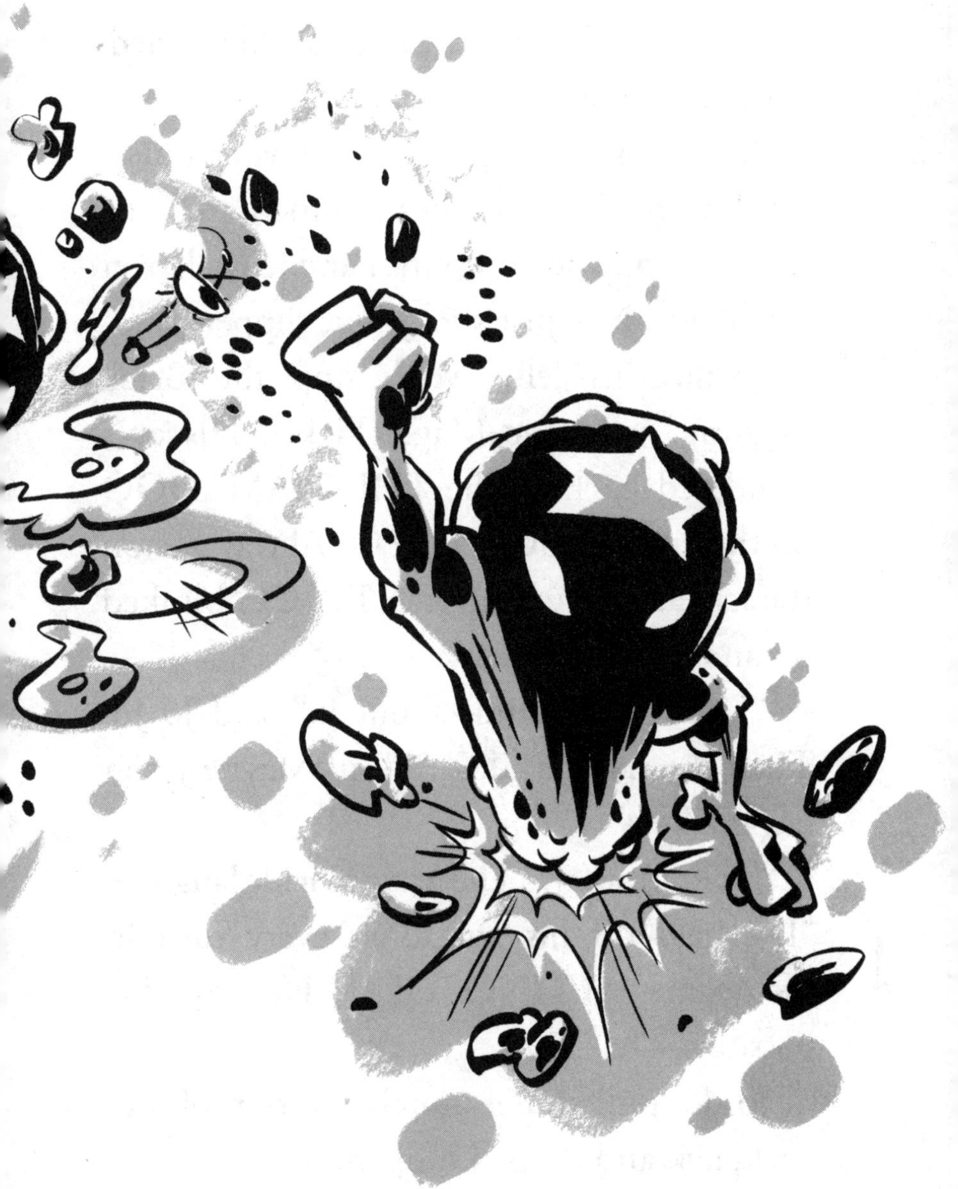

"Freedom!" the Magic Pickle cried. "You're a genius!"

Jo Jo blushed. "I just realized what a mess my PB and J sandwiches at lunch are," she said. "Drippy peanut butter and jelly all over my hands. Not just sticky, but slippery."

"Still, this jelly won't stop the Black Legume," said the Magic Pickle. His eyes wandered back to the THINGAMADOO on the ground. SCHNOZOLA! was still on the screen. The word CONTINUE? blinked on and off.

"Don't even think about it," said Jo Jo. Then she had an idea. "Wait! Maybe Jason has the key!"

"Your brother?" The Magic Pickle laughed. "I've held off his attacks at every turn in the game SCHNOZOLA! He couldn't possibly—"

Jo Jo pulled her notebook out of her backpack and flipped it open.

"Jason wrecked my notebook!" said Jo Jo. "He drew his goofy handkerchief guy and nose man all over it, but maybe there's a clue in his scribbling!"

Jo Jo showed the notebook to the Magic Pickle. On one page was a drawing of a big fist punching a big nose right in the middle,

between the nostrils. Jason's crummy drawing, but still, maybe a clue.

"The Nostrillain!" MP glared at the notebook. "Could it be that Jason is analyzing my maneuvers and compiling a series of notes on how to counteract my well-planned strikes?"

"Maybe, just maybe," said Jo Jo, "Jason finally did something useful and didn't even know it."

She picked up the THINGAMADOO and pressed CONTINUE.

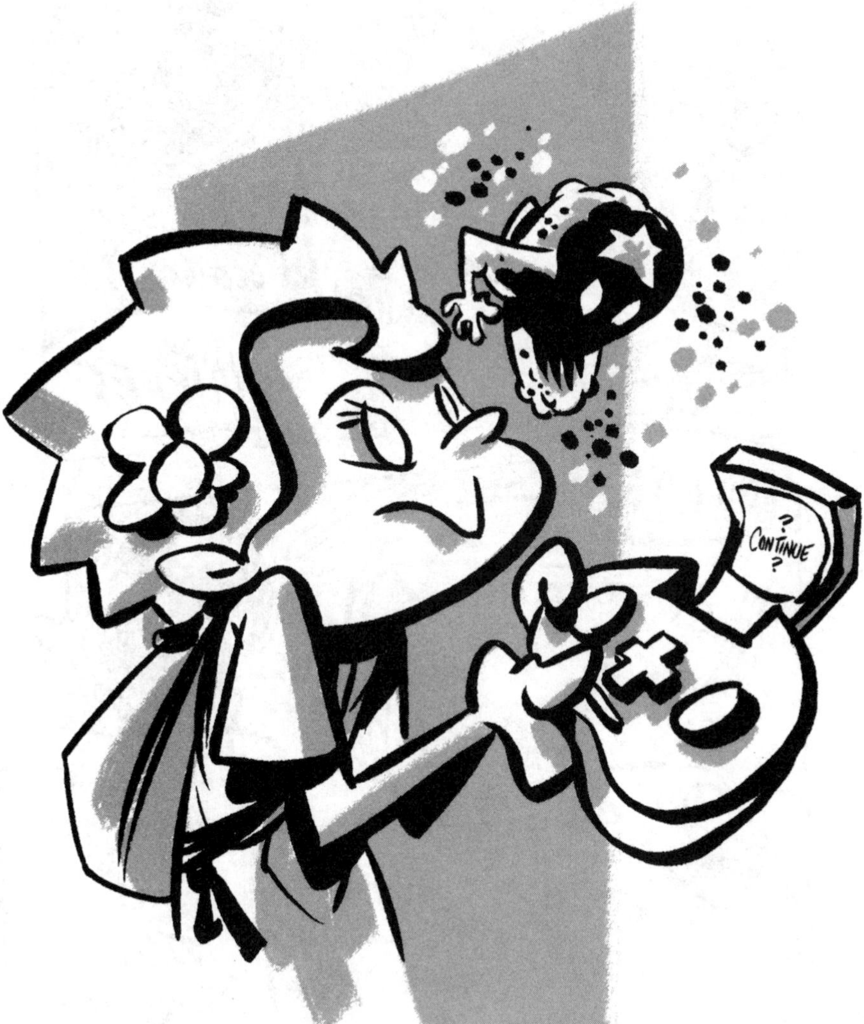
?
CONTINUE
?

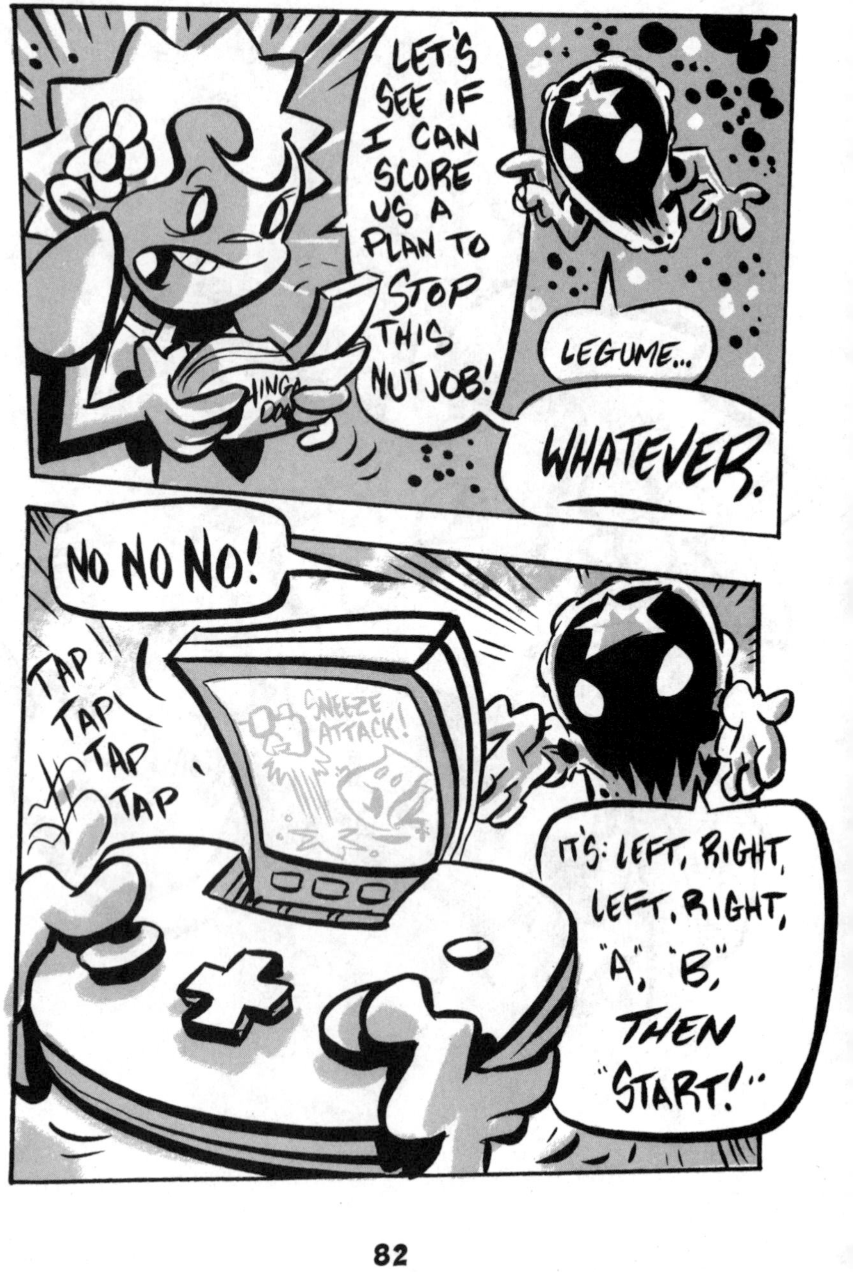
LET'S SEE IF I CAN SCORE US A PLAN TO STOP THIS NUTJOB!
LEGUME...
WHATEVER.
NO NO NO!
TAP TAP TAP TAP
SNEEZE ATTACK!
IT'S: LEFT, RIGHT, LEFT, RIGHT, "A", "B", THEN "START!"...

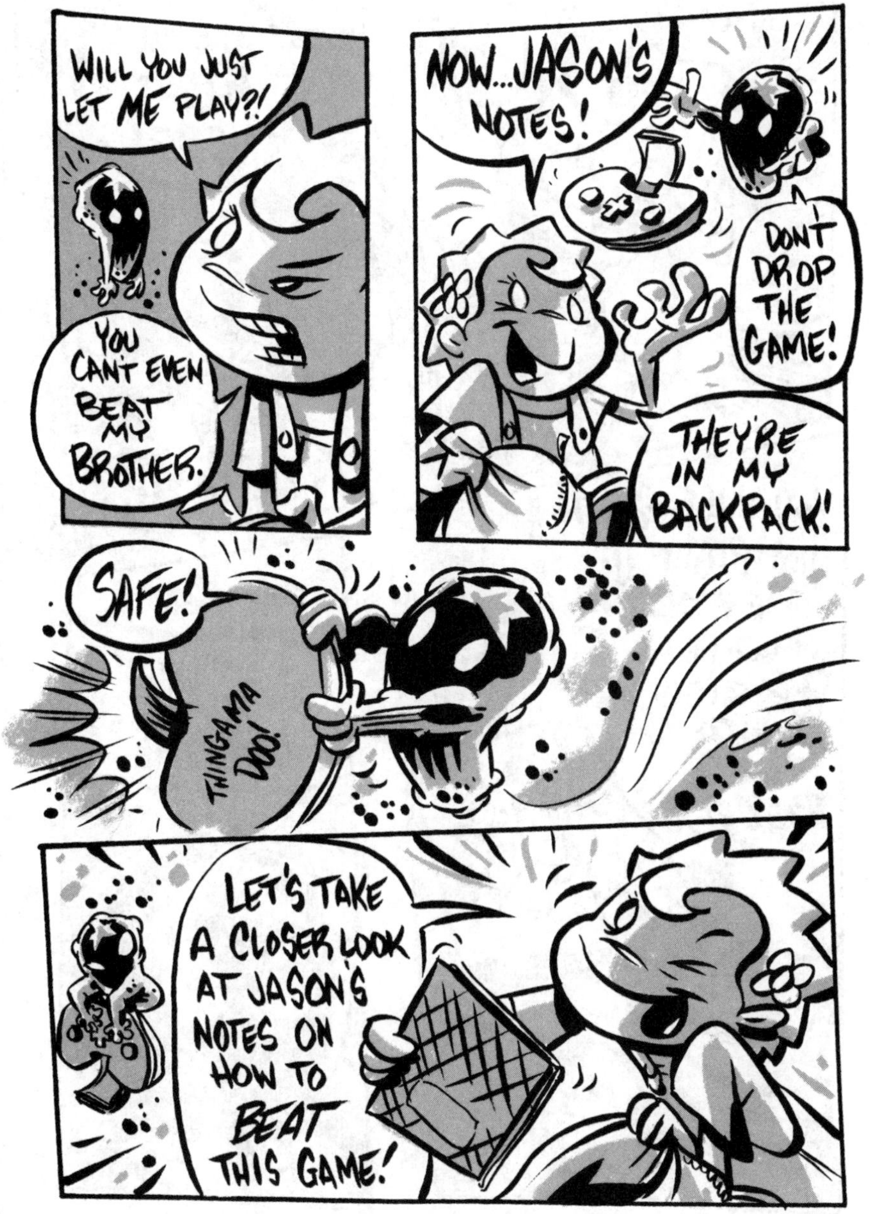
WILL YOU JUST LET ME PLAY?!
YOU CAN'T EVEN BEAT MY BROTHER.
NOW...JASON'S NOTES!
DON'T DROP THE GAME!
THEY'RE IN MY BACKPACK!
SAFE!
THINGAMA DOO!
LET'S TAKE A CLOSER LOOK AT JASON'S NOTES ON HOW TO BEAT THIS GAME!

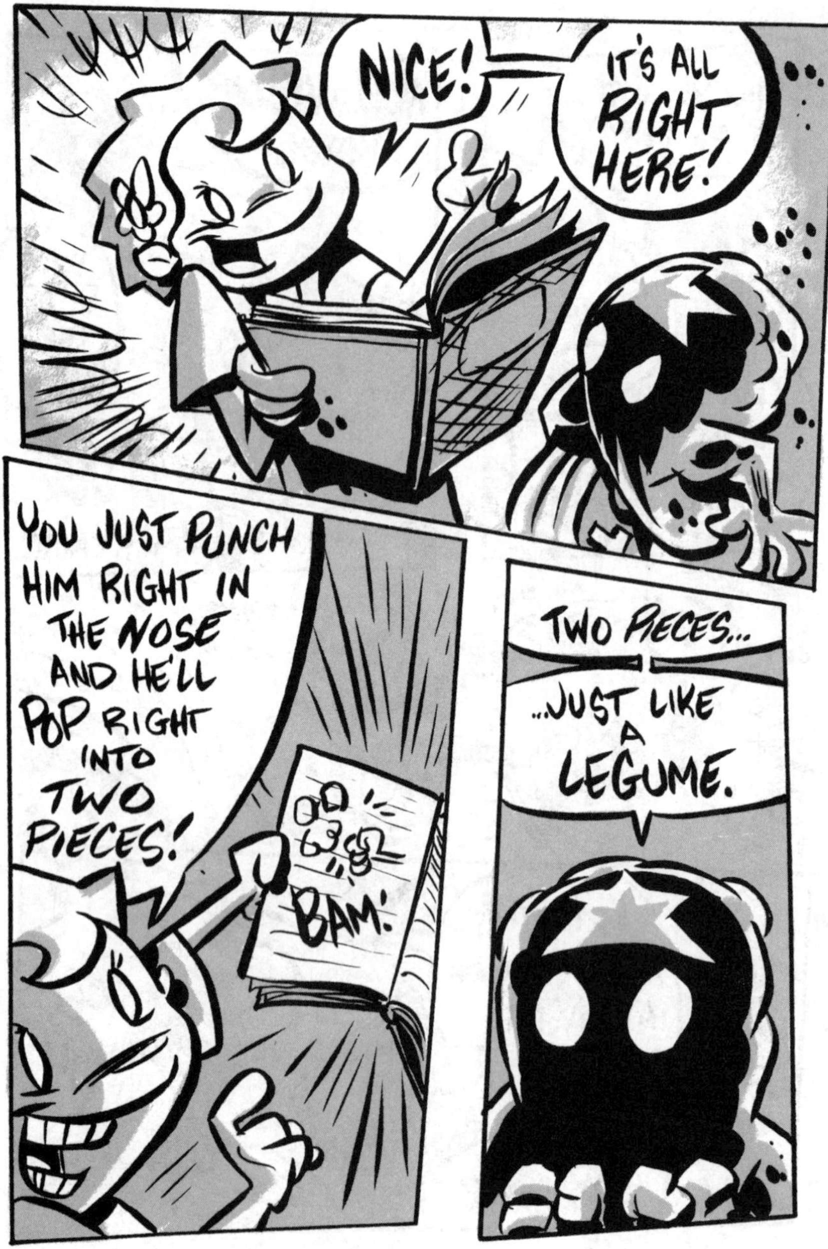
NICE!
IT'S ALL RIGHT HERE!
YOU JUST PUNCH HIM RIGHT IN THE NOSE AND HE'LL POP RIGHT INTO TWO PIECES!
BAM!
TWO PIECES...
...JUST LIKE A LEGUME.

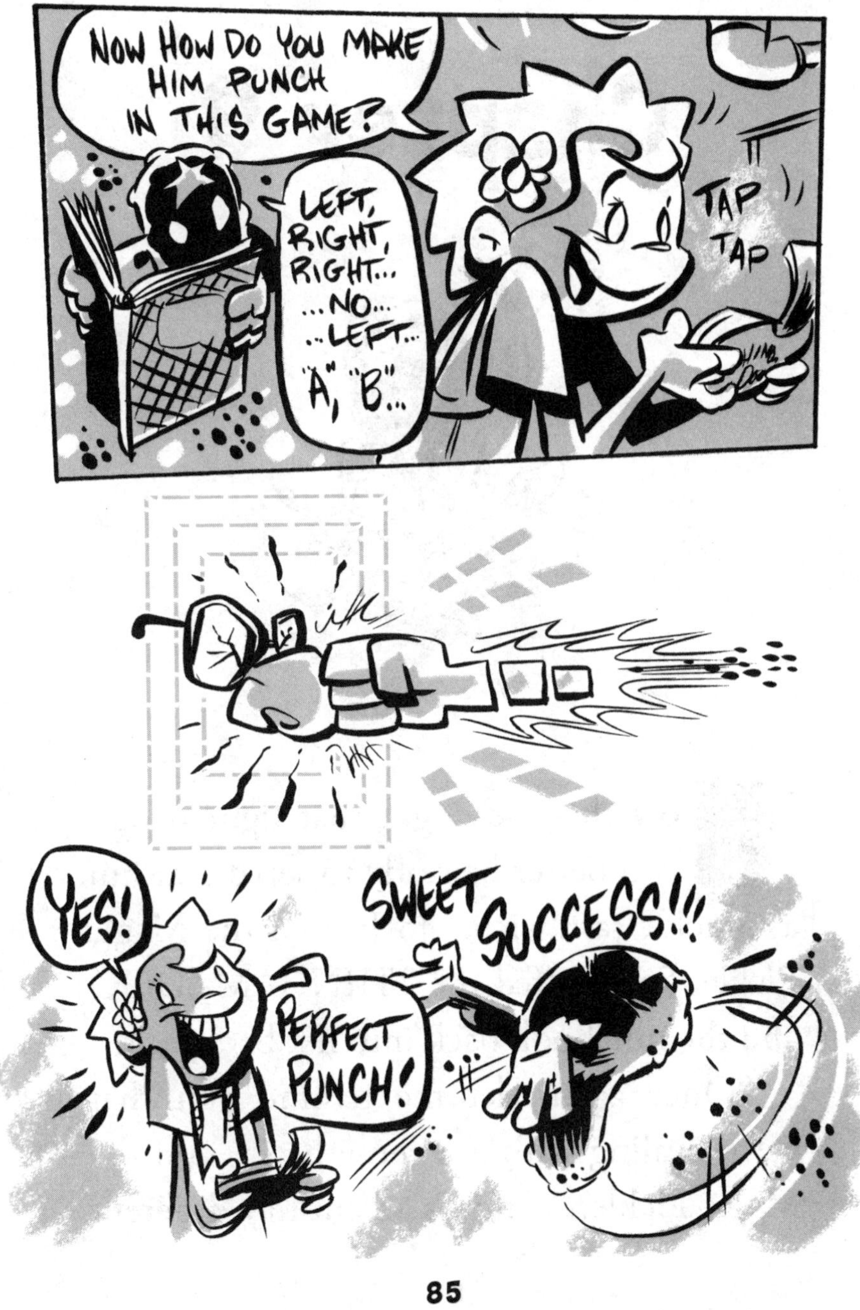
NOW HOW DO YOU MAKE HIM PUNCH IN THIS GAME?
LEFT, RIGHT, RIGHT... ...NO... ...LEFT... "A", "B"...
TAP TAP
YES!
SWEET SUCCESS!!!
PERFECT PUNCH!

# Chapter 9

"**N**ow that we've got that figured out, you better be ready to serve that nut a knuckle sandwich," Jo Jo told the Magic Pickle. She stuffed the THINGAMADOO and the notebook back into her backpack.

"Once again, let me remind you that we're dealing with a legume here," said the Magic Pickle. "A nut is an entirely different

can of beans."

"What?" Jo Jo giggled.

MP winked. "You know what I mean," he said. "The good news is that you've freed me from my constricting prison of peanut butter by using the jelly."

"Yeah, I'm a genius," Jo Jo replied.

"I applaud your ingenuity," said MP as

he saluted. "Perhaps you should begin the task of freeing the others encased in peanut butter? Your teacher and fellow academic comrades?"

"I thought about that," answered Jo Jo. "But you know, if we free them too early, they'll see the Black Legume, and they'll see you, and they'll see me talking to you and helping to fight the Creature, and then I'll have to explain things, and then they'll all want your autograph, and—"

"I see your point," said the Magic Pickle. "Operation under cover of peanut butter may work to our advantage, at least as far as staying top secret. Excellent call."

"Again, I'm a genius," said Jo Jo.

"And again, I salute your ingenuity," said MP.

## FWOOOSH!

With a flash of green, he flew off into the depths of the Mixing Facility.

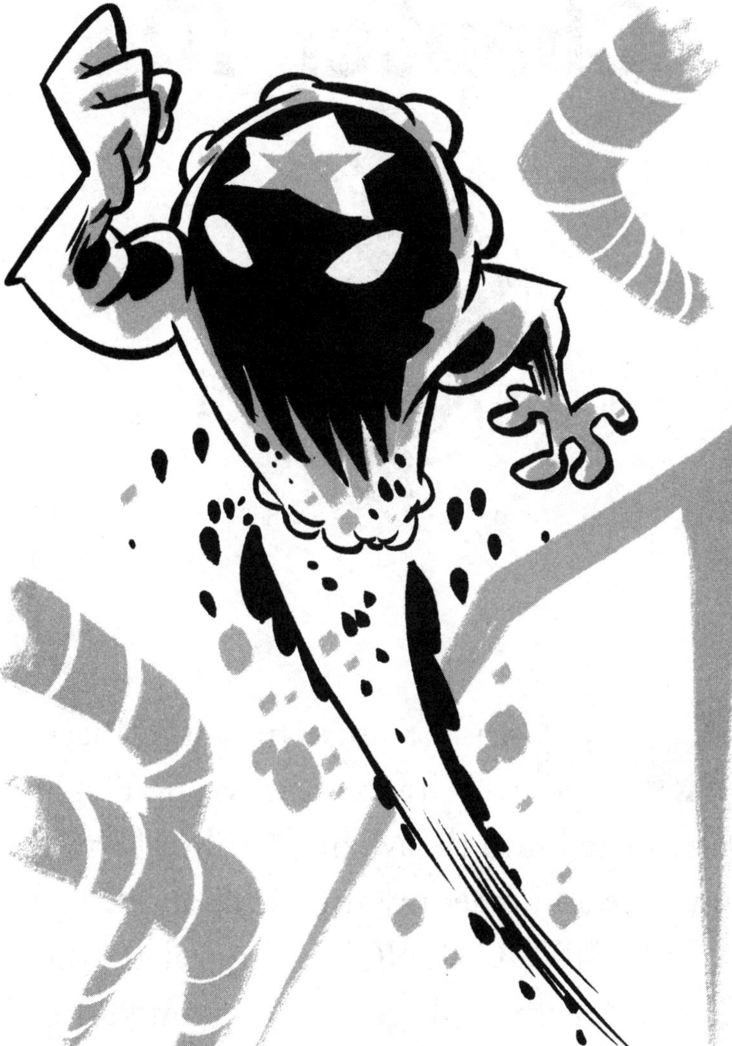

# Chapter 10

"Step forth, Creature from the Black Legume!" shouted the Magic Pickle as he soared into the Mixing Facility. "Show your face and meet my fist with honor!"

"NUTTY CRUNCH!" squealed the Creature with evil glee. He pointed his fingers like a fire hose filled with gooey peanut butter and let loose.

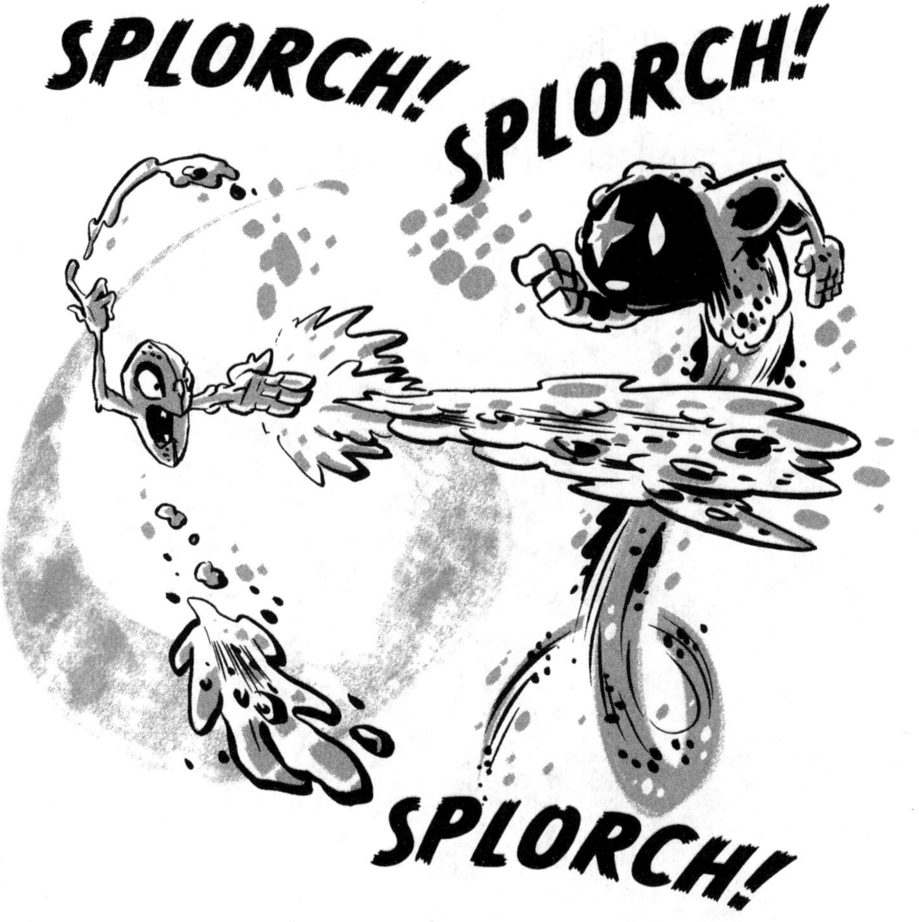
SPLORCH!
SPLORCH!
SPLORCH!

Stream after soupy stream of peanut butter blasted through the air, aimed at the Magic Pickle. MP circled like a fighter jet, narrowly avoiding every last bit of gloppy chunkiness.

“You’ll have to goo better than that,” warned the Magic Pickle. He pointed his hand at an oncoming glob of Nutty Crunch.

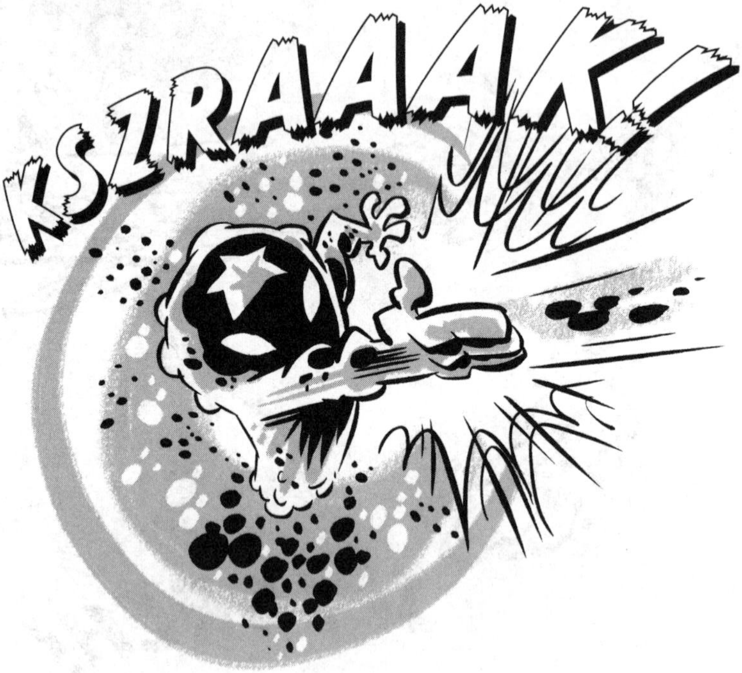
KSZRAAAK!

The peanut butter glob fried in midair, burnt to a crisp.

“Nothing like a roasted peanut.” The Magic Pickle laughed. “Now, if only I had some salt . . .”

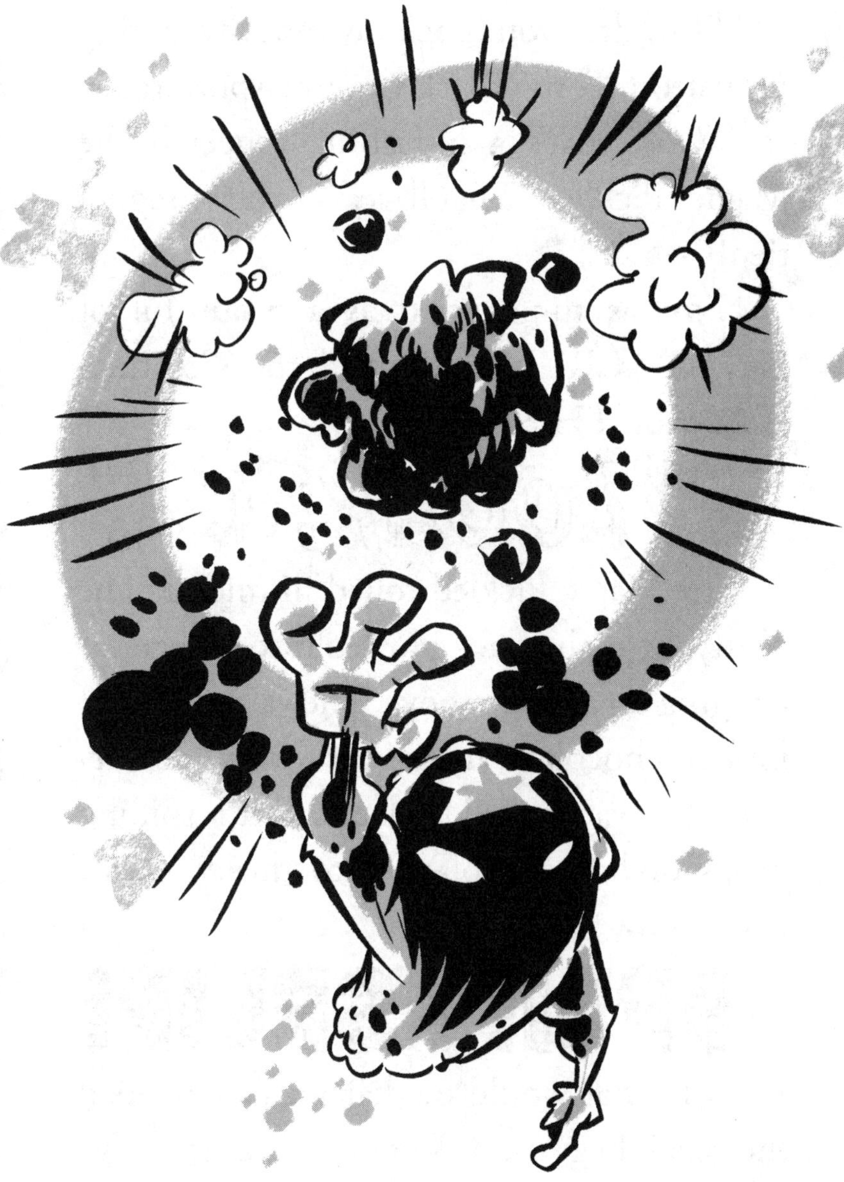

"How dare you mock my mouthwatering maelstrom?!" the Black Legume sputtered.

"Wow, that's a mouthful," sneered the Magic Pickle. "That'll leave you tongue-tied!"

"Not as tongue-tied as a mouthful of NUTTY CRUNCH!" cried the Creature. "Chew on THIS!"

## SPLOOARRCH!

The Magic Pickled rolled in midair. The Nutty Crunch attack plowed into a huge vat hanging on a hinge above. The vat was full of molten chocolate, meant for forming candy bars. The vat rocked back and forth, spilling drops of hot chocolate onto the conveyor belt below.

## SPLIP! SPLIP!

"Oh, that would be delicious!" chuckled the Black Legume. "What an idea! After I've

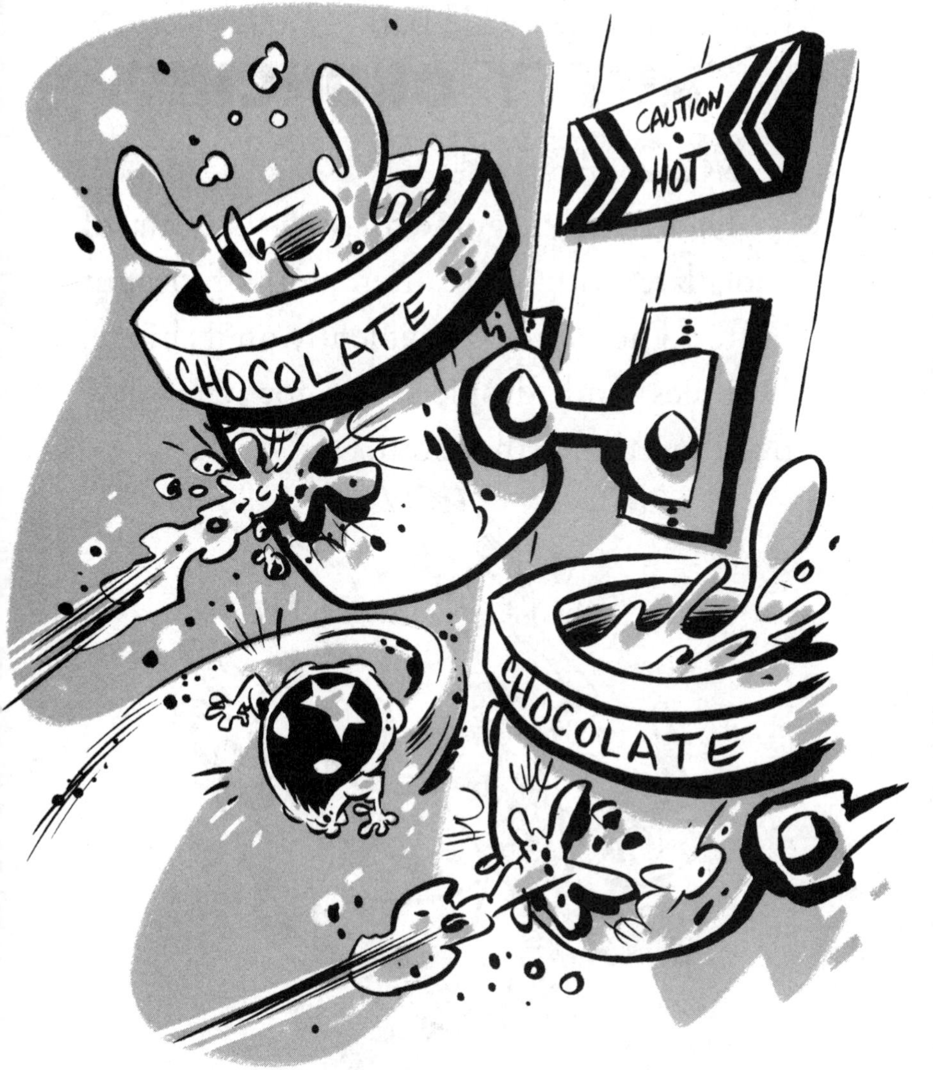
CAUTION
HOT
CHOCOLATE
CHOCOLATE

defeated you, I'll mold you into the world's first Chocolate Pickle Bar!"

## "NUTTY CRUNCH!"

### SPLOOARRCH! SPLOOARRCH!

The Black Legume blasted the vat of chocolate with glob after glob of peanut butter. The vat rocked violently on its hinge. Dribbles and droplets of hot chocolate overflowed into the room.

The Magic Pickle stopped and watched. The Creature was obsessed; his complete attention was on the vat of chocolate! Now was MP's chance!

In a powerful burst of green lightning, the Magic Pickle flew at the Creature, flying fists forced forward.

"NOOO!!!" wailed the Black Legume as the Magic Pickle landed the perfect punch.

## SNAP!!! THLURP!!!

The Black Legume snapped in two down the middle, each half falling, falling into a chocolate pool.

MP zoomed over to a heat lamp and switched it on at full power.

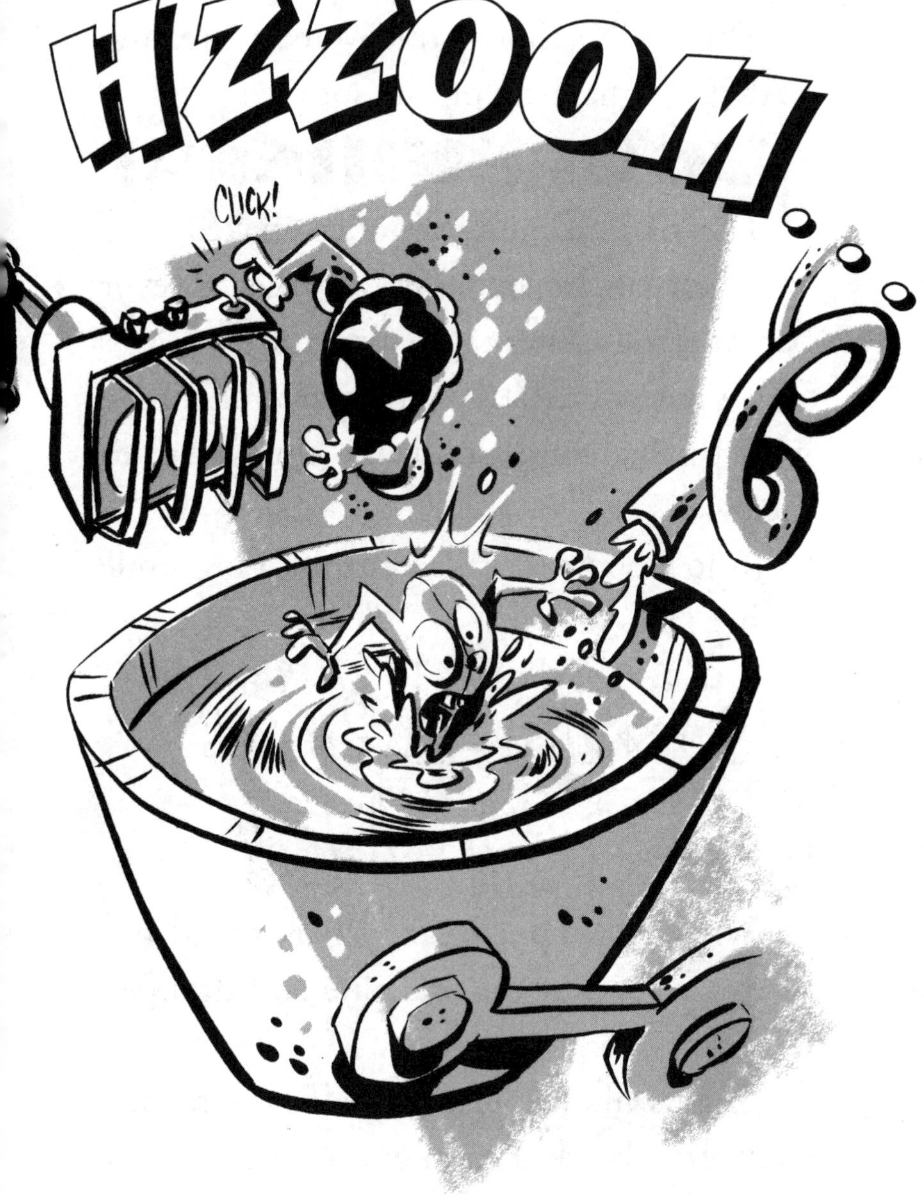
HZZOOM
CLICK!

The evil, chocolate-covered Creature BAKED right there on the spot!

## BOOP! WHIRRR!

The Black Legume, broken, baked, and smothered in chocolate, fell onto the conveyor belt and rolled away into a machine.

"What? How?" MP spun around to see why the machine suddenly chugged into life.

Jo Jo stood near the controls, a big smile on her face.

A neatly wrapped candy bar rattled out of the far end of the machine and dropped onto the floor.

"Looks like we just turned the Creature from the Black Legume into the Candy

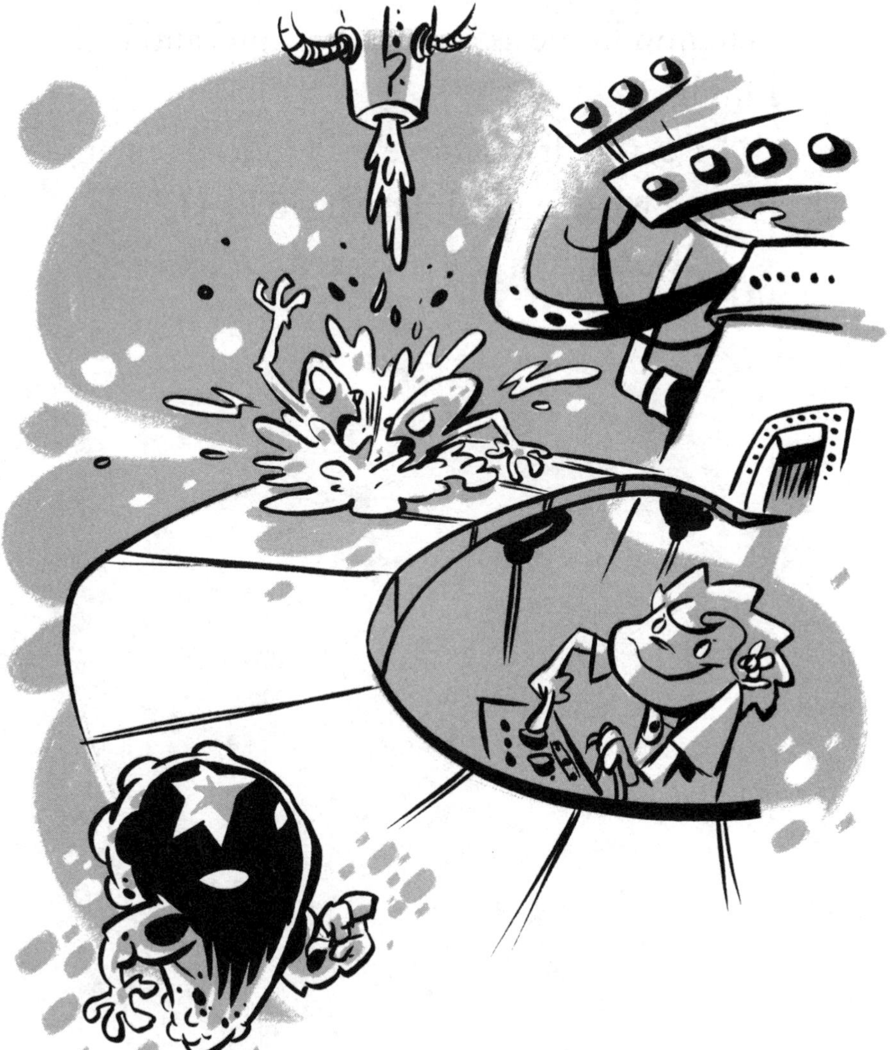

from the Black Legume," said Jo Jo. "Let's take him home as our 'free sample' and lock him up."

"Yes, this 'free sample' will indeed remain behind bars," agreed the Magic Pickle.

"*Candy* bars!" Jo Jo winked.

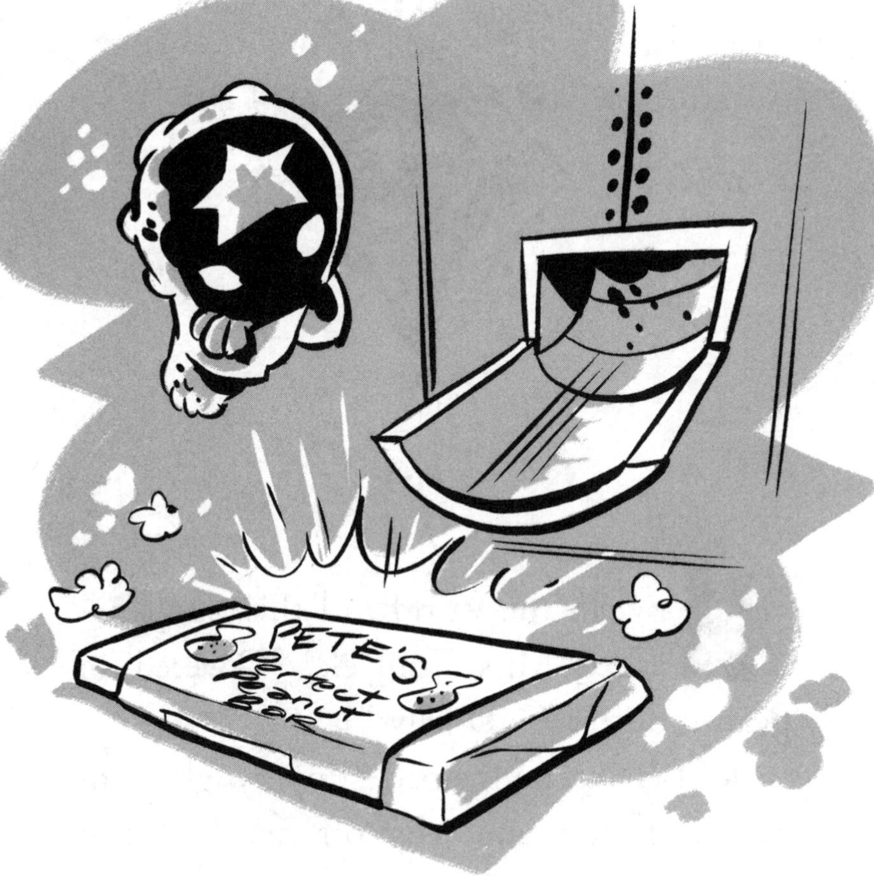
PETE'S
Perfect
Peanut
BAR

# Chapter 11

"How in the world did this happen?" asked Miss Emilyek. "Covered in peanut butter AND jelly?"

Jo Jo's teacher wiped slippery globs of peanut butter and jelly off her face and looked around. Her entire class and every worker in PETE'S PERFECT PEANUTS factory were doing the same thing.

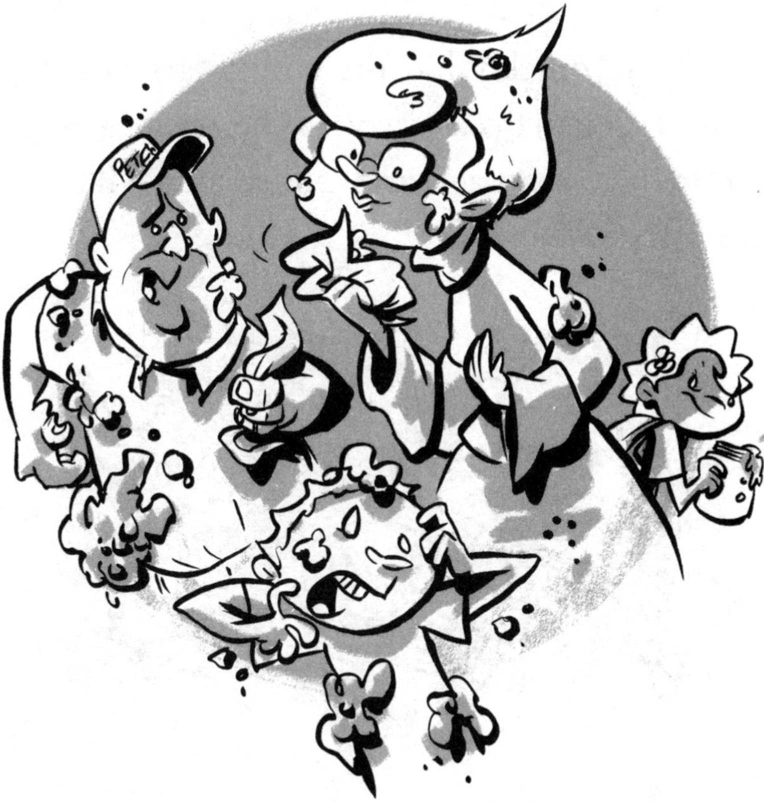
PETE'S

"Musta been some kinda malfunction," a factory worker guessed. "Looks like our Tasting Facility went kablooey, too. Peanut butter and jelly everywhere!"

"I feel like lunch!" said Mikey. "Hey, where's my THINGAMADOO? I hope it's not all globbed up!"

Jo Jo quickly hid the empty jars of jelly she'd used to free everyone. Then she reached into her backpack and pulled out Mikey's THINGAMADOO.

"This thing is AWESOME!" Jo Jo said. "Just make sure you smack the Nostrillain square in the nose or you'll blow it."

"You'll blow his NOSE?" asked Mikey.

"No, the GAME," Jo Jo replied.

"I just hope we still get our free candy bars!" Ellen chimed in.

"Yeah," said Jo Jo. "I should probably grab one for Jason, too."

"You're gonna give a free candy bar to your BROTHER?!" cried Ellen. "What did HE do to deserve that kind of present?"

"He let me borrow his notes," answered Jo Jo.

# Chapter 12

"I'm glad that's over with," the Magic Pickle said. He pressed a button on his crime-computer keyboard; a grid appeared on the screen. The notorious members of the Brotherhood of Evil Produce appeared in boxes. Some had big red *X*s across their faces; others still grinned their evil grins. These veggie villains were out there, somewhere at large, awaiting their fair share of dill justice.

**BOOP!**

A big red *X* sliced its way through the face of the Creature from the Black Legume like a knife through a loaf of bread.

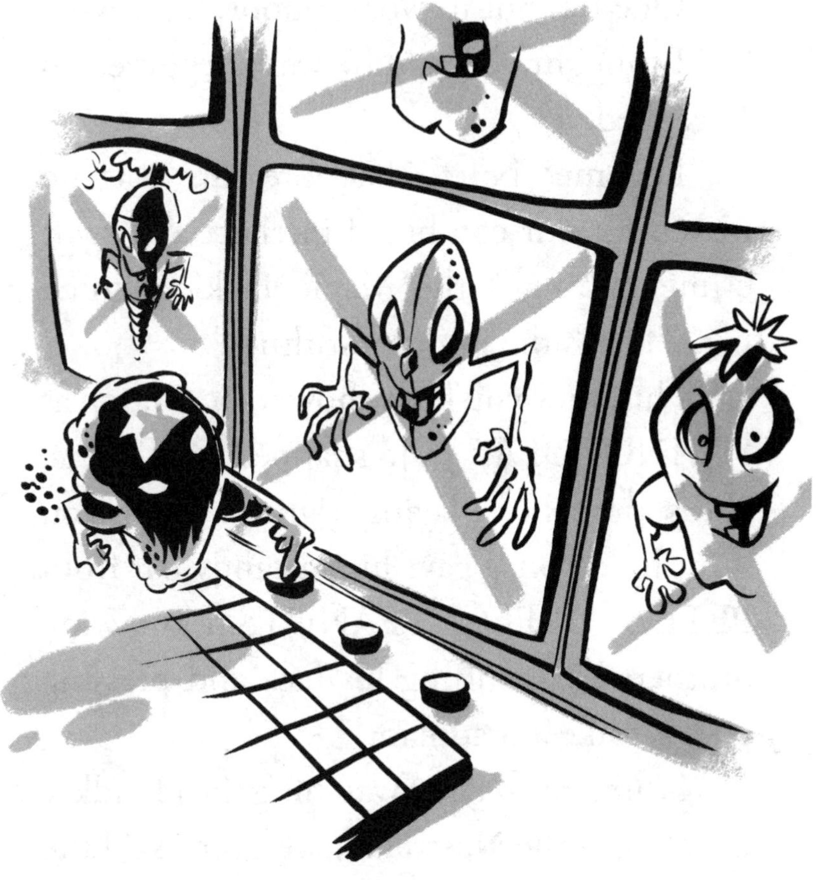

"I relish moments like this," said the Magic Pickle. He proudly looked up at a framed candy bar hanging on the wall. A trophy from the day: the chocolaty prison of the Black Legume.

"One less nut to worry about," said MP.

"I thought you said he was a legume," Jo Jo replied.

"Legume? Nut? That Creature was no match for our combined intellect and swift crime fighting," the Magic Pickle assured her. "That's the important thing."

"Plus, now you know how to beat Jason at SCHNOZOLA!" Jo Jo snapped her fingers. "He's probably playing right now, if you want to log on. I gave him a candy bar from PETE'S PERFECT PEANUTS. I know my brother: He's stuffing his face and pressing buttons like a madman."

"I think my days of watching the Handker Chief fight the Nostrillain are over," said the

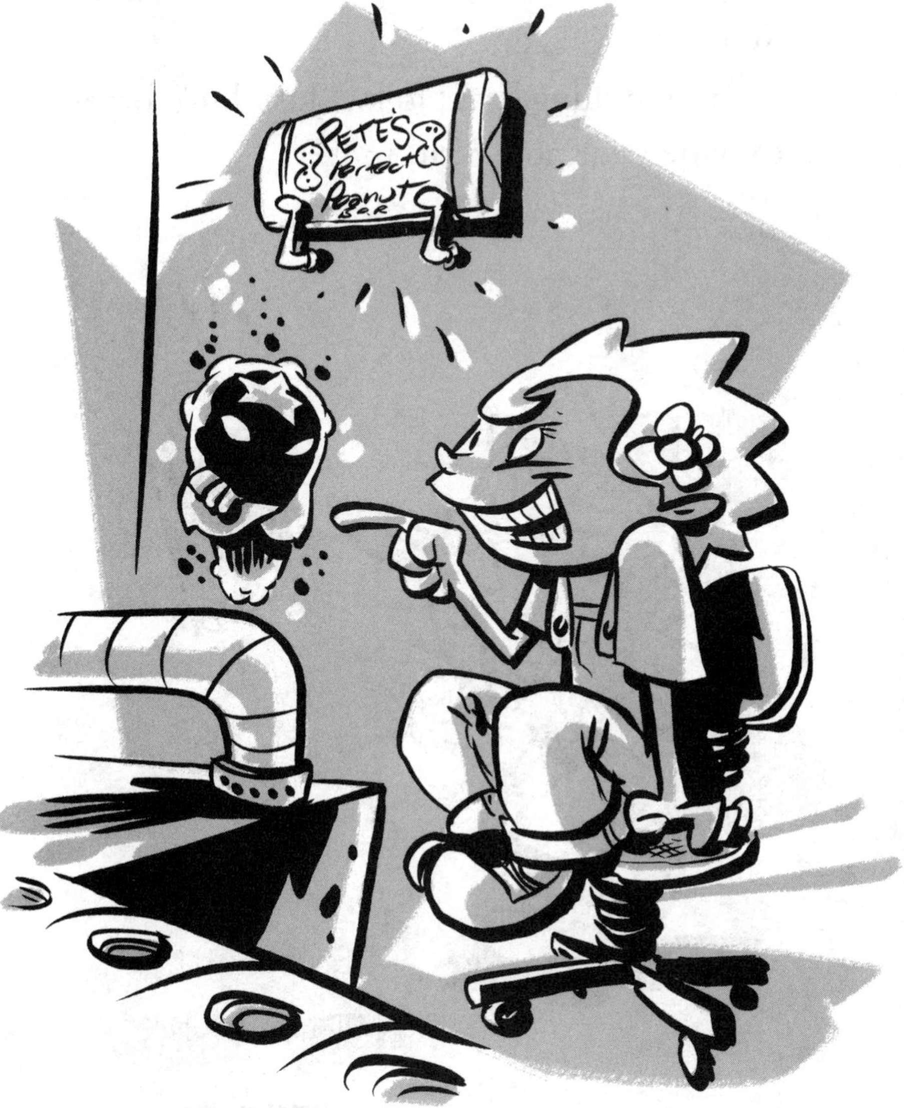
PETE'S
Perfect
Peanut
BAR

Magic Pickle. "I'm washing my hands of SCHNOZOLA!"

"Good thing," said Jo Jo. "Just don't forget to wipe your nose of it, too!"

**THE END**

# BONUS STORY!!!

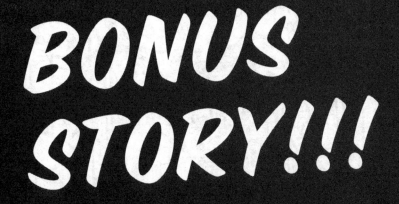

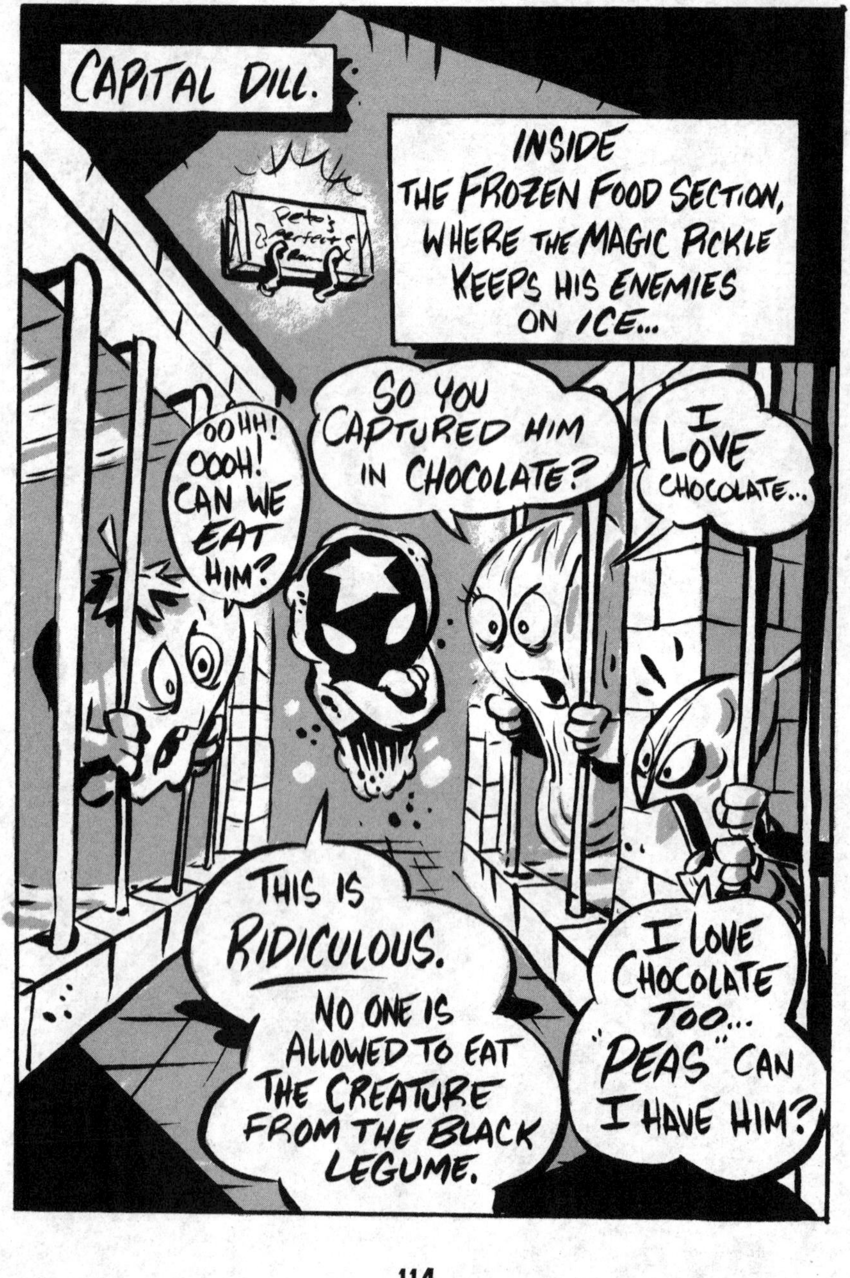
CAPITAL DILL.
INSIDE THE FROZEN FOOD SECTION, WHERE THE MAGIC PICKLE KEEPS HIS ENEMIES ON ICE...
OOHH! OOOH! CAN WE EAT HIM?
SO YOU CAPTURED HIM IN CHOCOLATE?
I LOVE CHOCOLATE...
THIS IS RIDICULOUS. NO ONE IS ALLOWED TO EAT THE CREATURE FROM THE BLACK LEGUME.
I LOVE CHOCOLATE TOO... "PEAS" CAN I HAVE HIM?

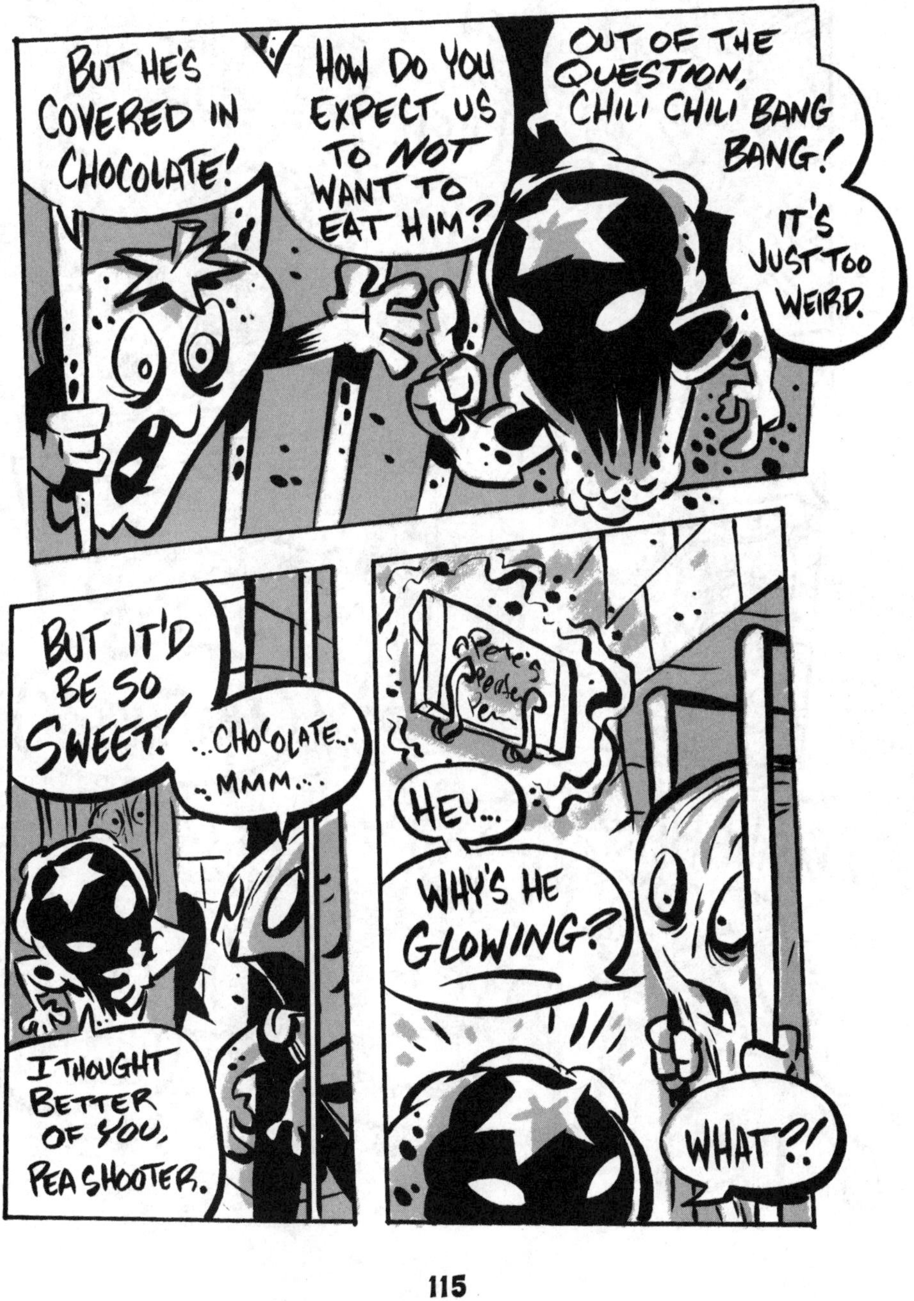
BUT HE'S COVERED IN CHOCOLATE!
HOW DO YOU EXPECT US TO NOT WANT TO EAT HIM?
OUT OF THE QUESTION, CHILI CHILI BANG BANG!
IT'S JUST TOO WEIRD.
BUT IT'D BE SO SWEET!
...CHOCOLATE... ...MMM...
I THOUGHT BETTER OF YOU, PEASHOOTER.
HEY...
WHY'S HE GLOWING?
WHAT?!

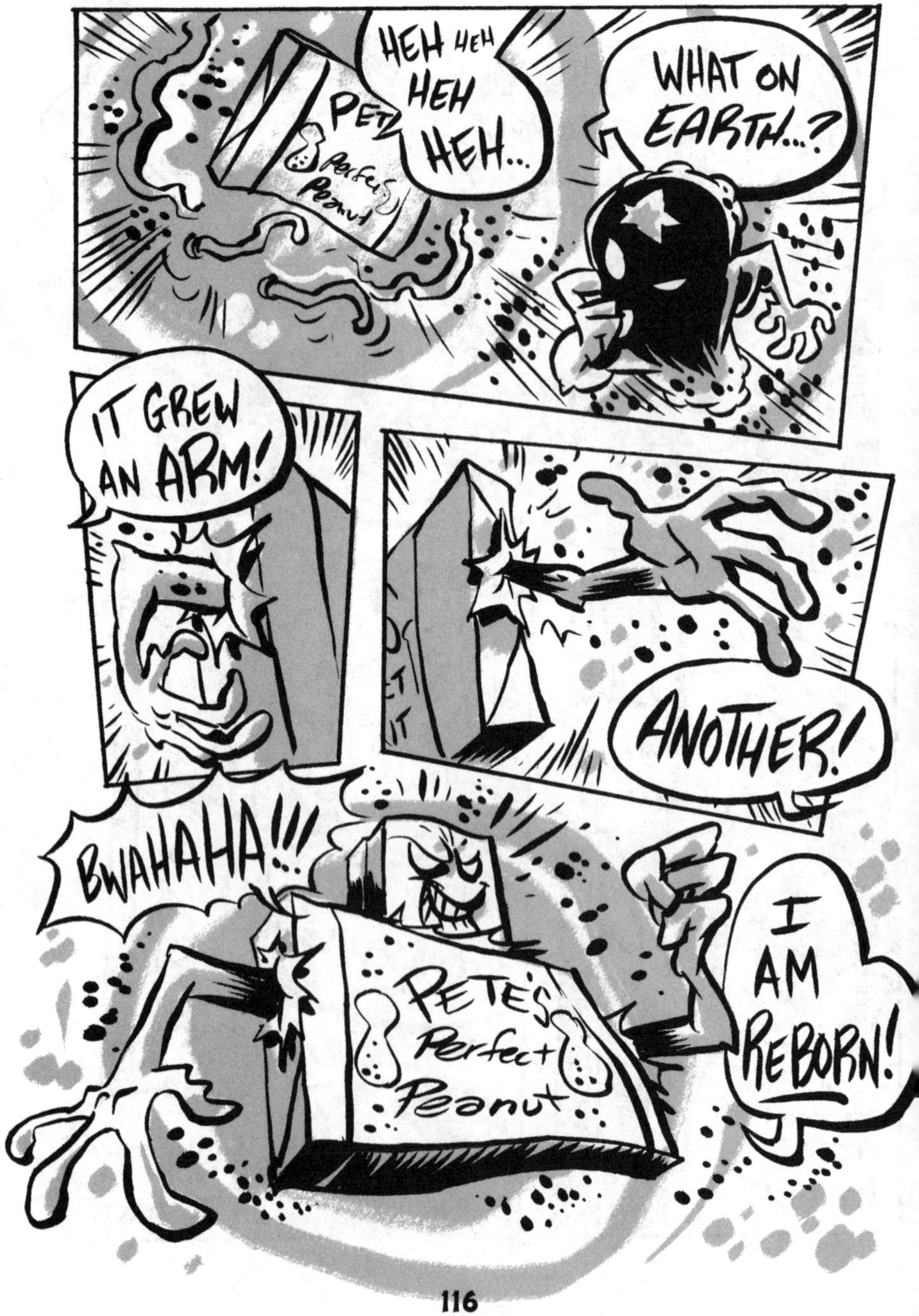
HEH HEH HEH HEH...
PETE'S Perfect Peanut
WHAT ON EARTH...?
IT GREW AN ARM!
ANOTHER!
BWAHAHA!!!
PETE'S Perfect Peanut
I AM REBORN!

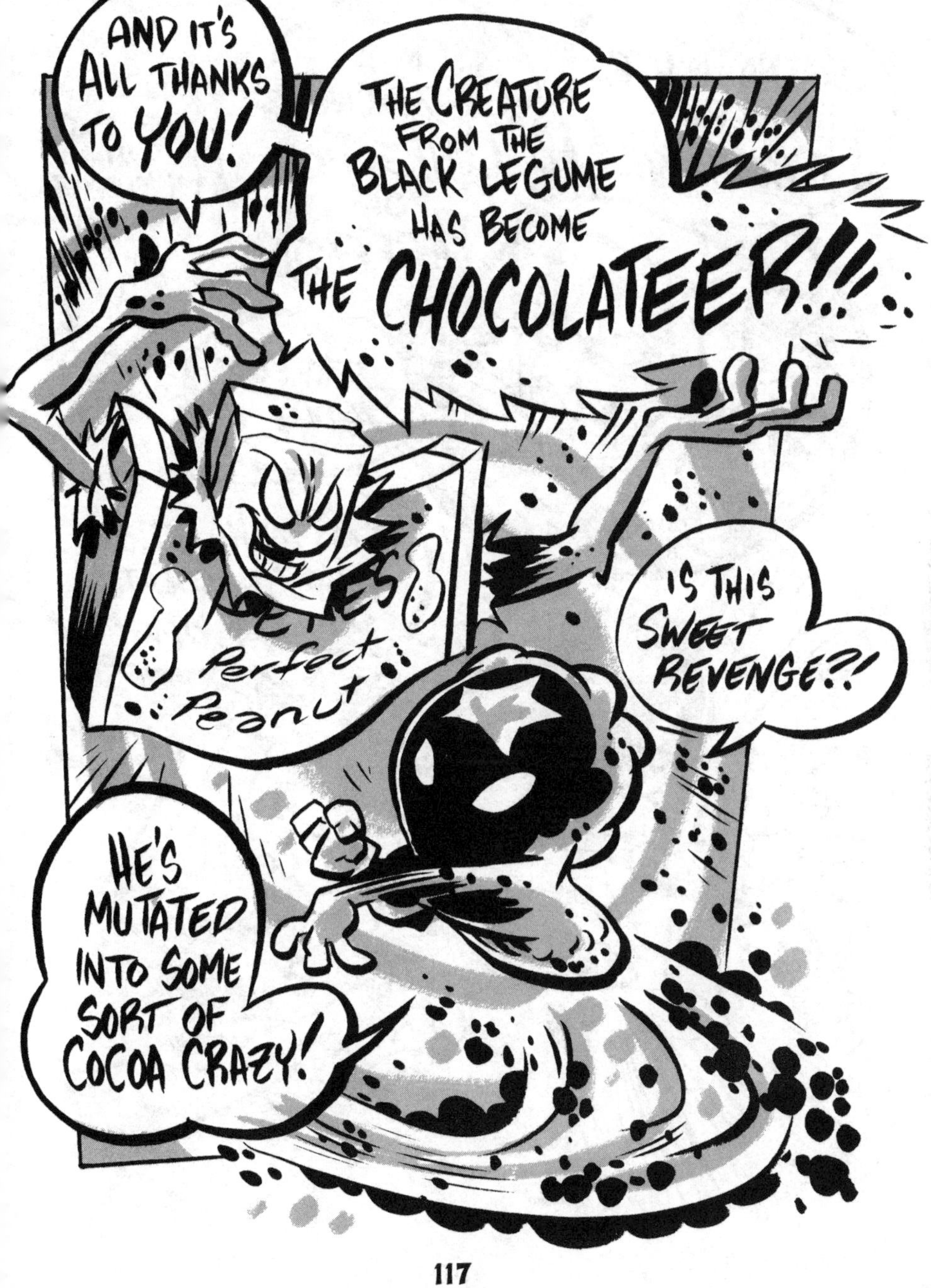
AND IT'S ALL THANKS TO YOU!
THE CREATURE FROM THE BLACK LEGUME HAS BECOME THE CHOCOLATEER!!!
Perfect Peanut
IS THIS SWEET REVENGE?!
HE'S MUTATED INTO SOME SORT OF COCOA CRAZY!

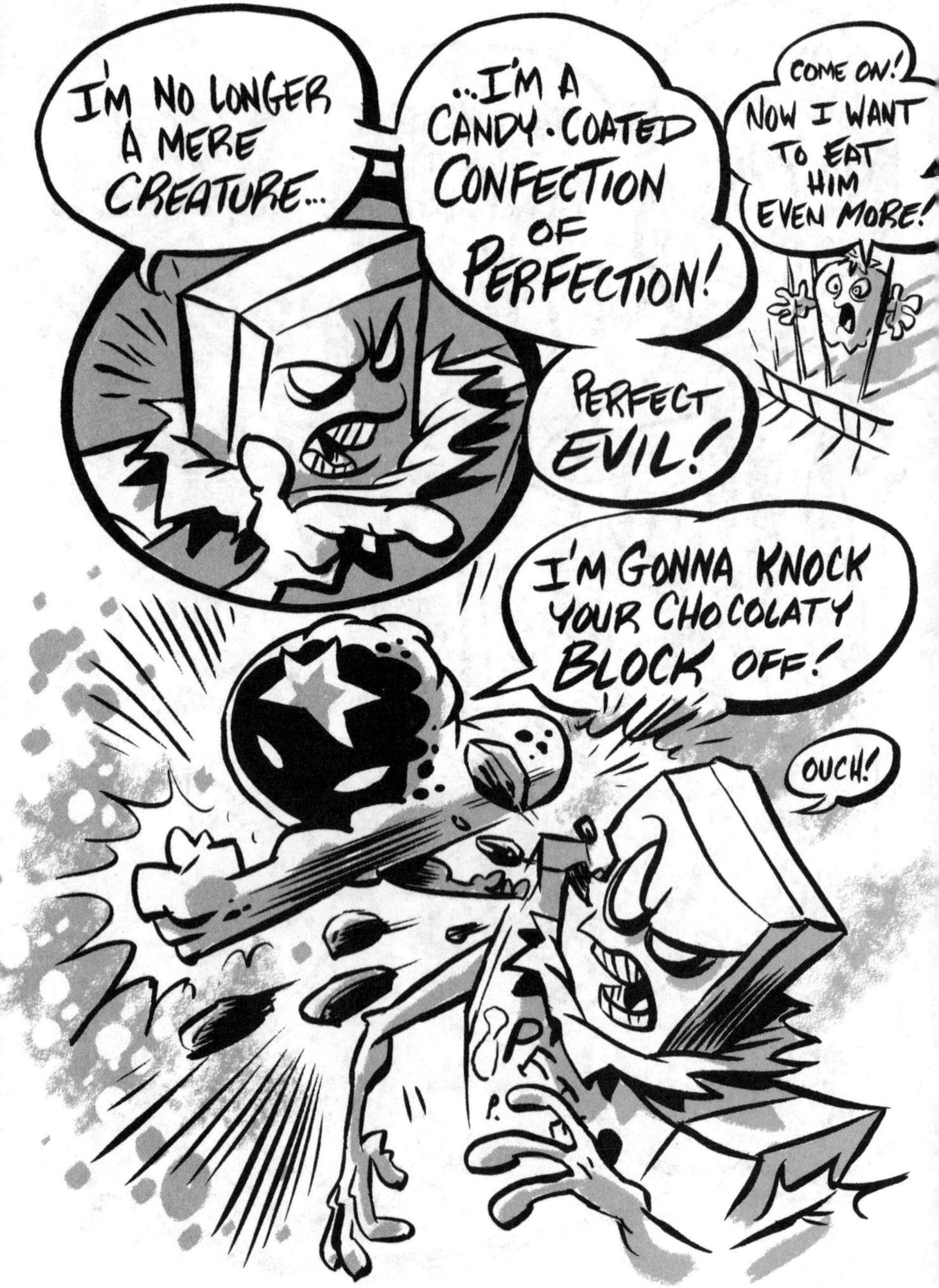
I'M NO LONGER A MERE CREATURE...
...I'M A CANDY-COATED CONFECTION OF PERFECTION!
COME ON! NOW I WANT TO EAT HIM EVEN MORE!
PERFECT EVIL!
I'M GONNA KNOCK YOUR CHOCOLATY BLOCK OFF!
OUCH!
P.
P.

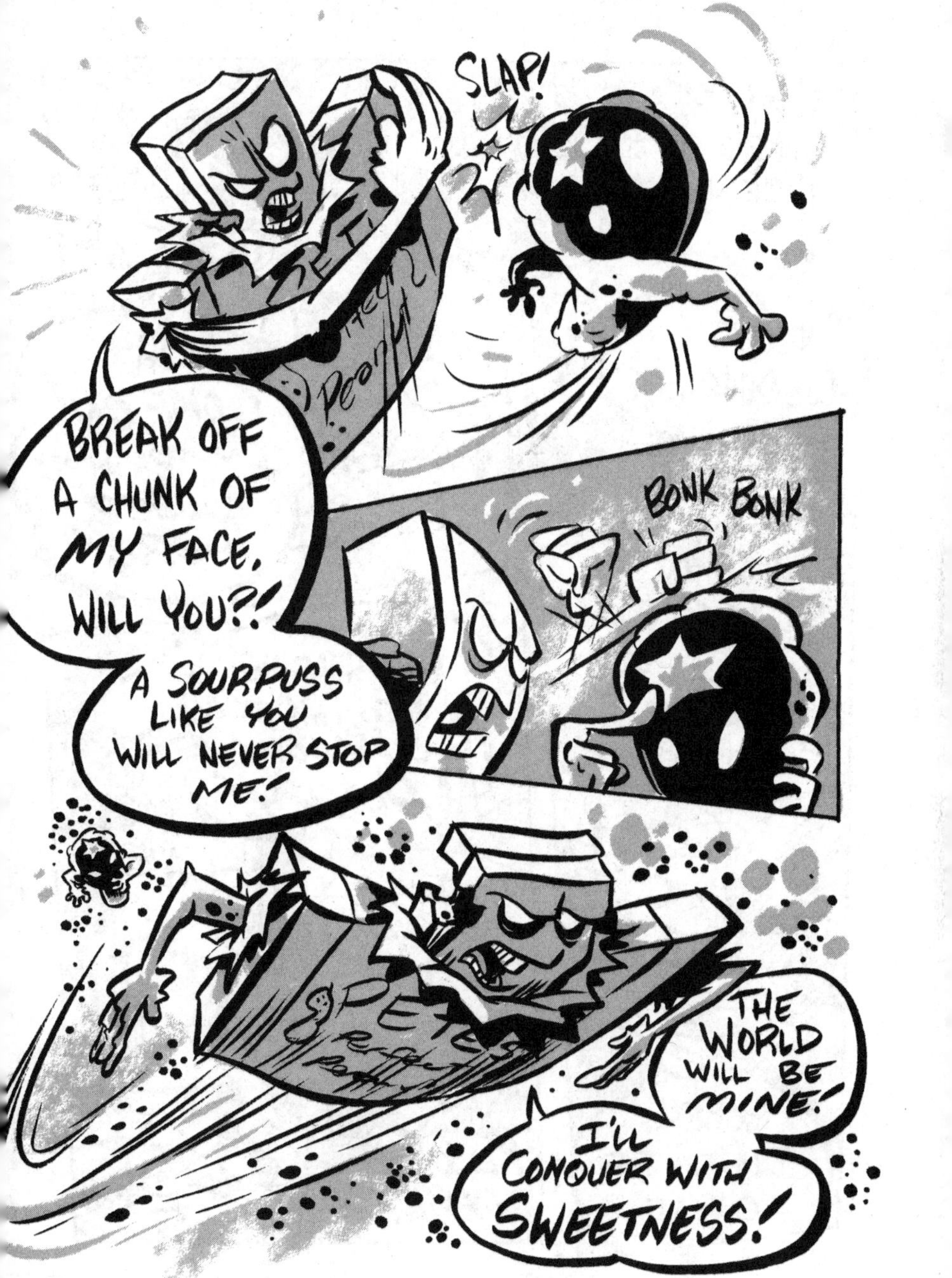

SLAP!
BREAK OFF A CHUNK OF MY FACE, WILL YOU?!
A SOURPUSS LIKE YOU WILL NEVER STOP ME!
BONK BONK
THE WORLD WILL BE MINE!
I'LL CONQUER WITH SWEETNESS!

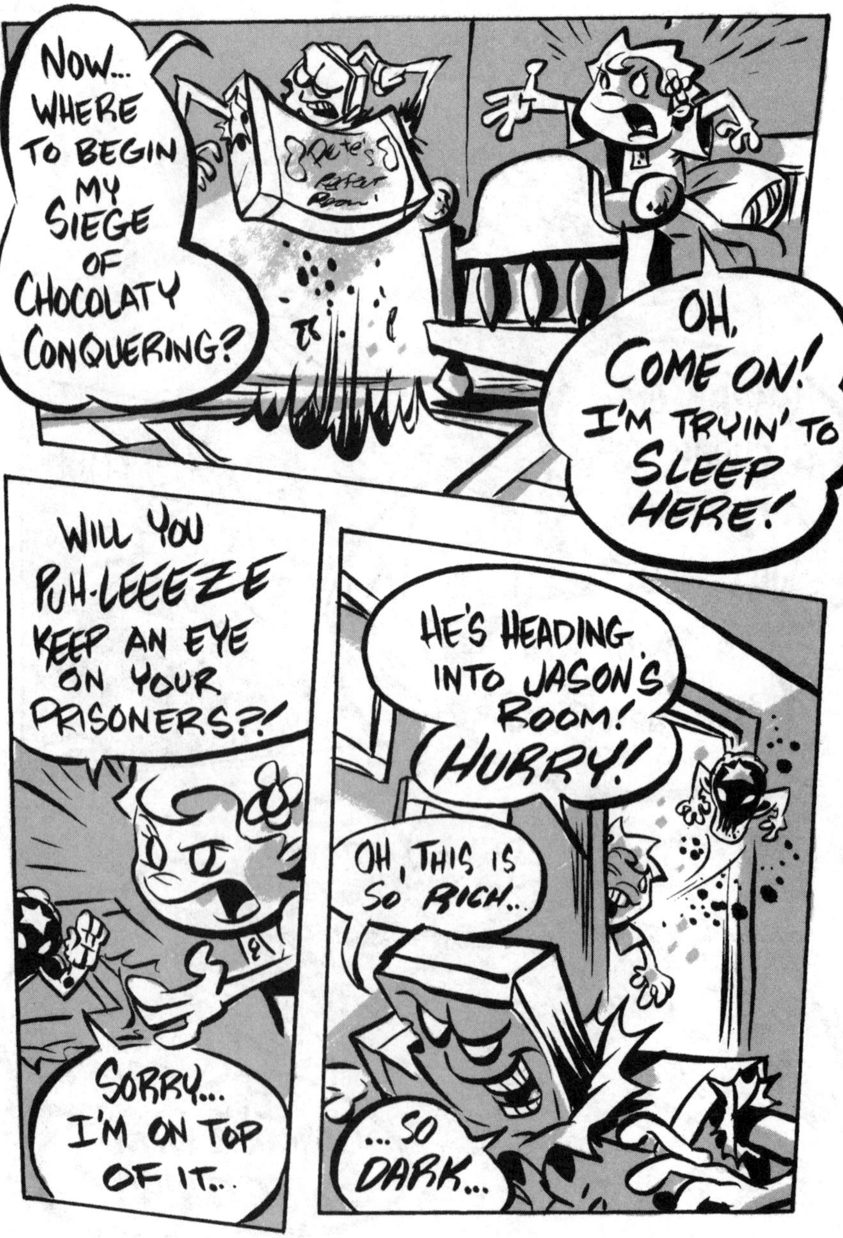

NOW... WHERE TO BEGIN MY SIEGE OF CHOCOLATY CONQUERING?
OH, COME ON! I'M TRYIN' TO SLEEP HERE!
WILL YOU PUH-LEEEZE KEEP AN EYE ON YOUR PRISONERS?!
SORRY... I'M ON TOP OF IT...
HE'S HEADING INTO JASON'S ROOM! HURRY!
OH, THIS IS SO RICH...
... SO DARK...

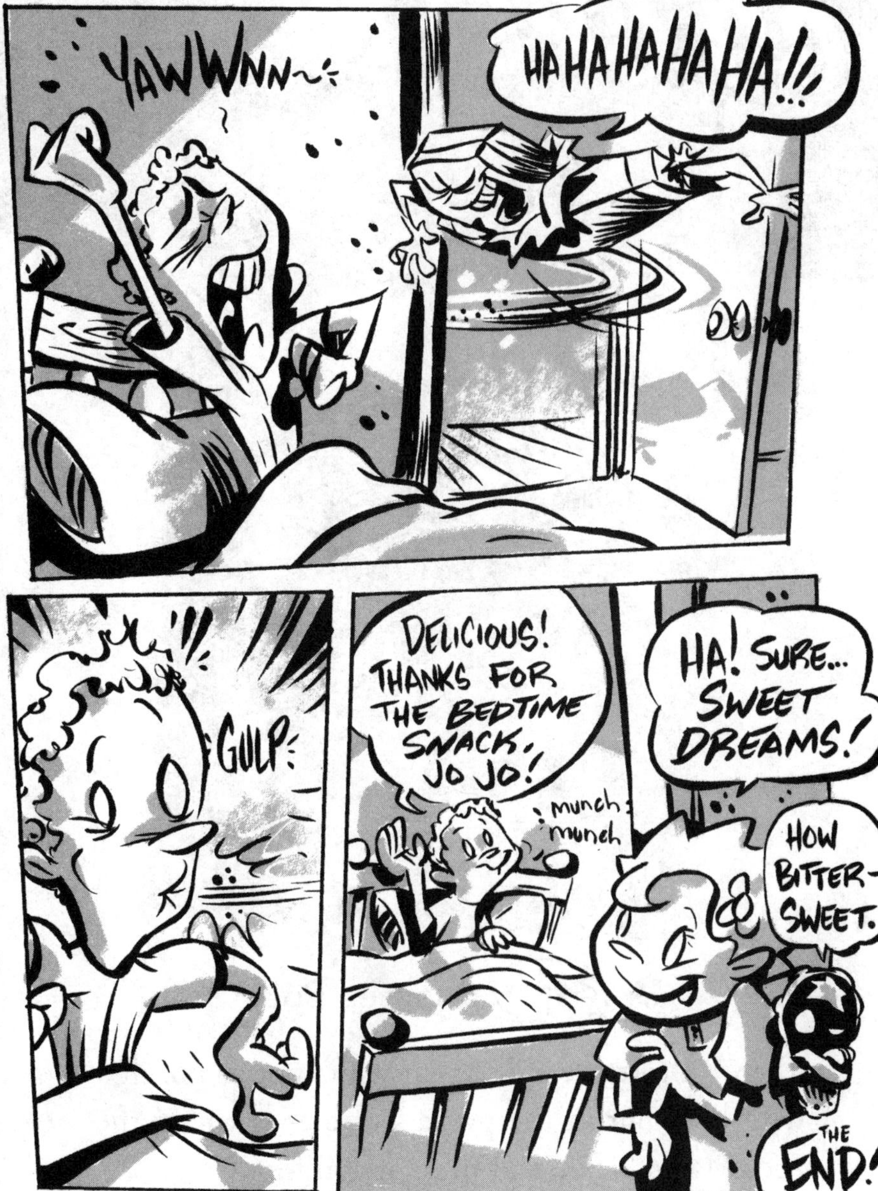
YAWWNN~
HAHAHAHAHAHA!!!
GULP
DELICIOUS! THANKS FOR THE BEDTIME SNACK, JO JO!
munch munch
HA! SURE... SWEET DREAMS!
HOW BITTER-SWEET.
THE END!

# GO GREEN!

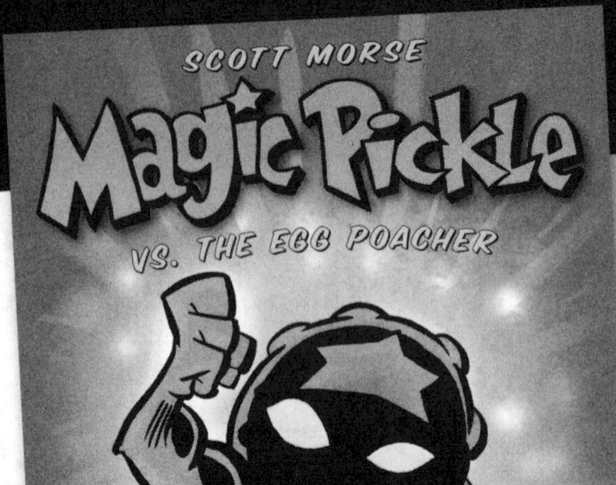
SCOTT MORSE
Magic Pickle
VS. THE EGG POACHER
SCHOLASTIC

A graphix Chapter Book

There's a rotten egg in town who's out to poach a wild kiwi but in the process creates havoc at the zoo. Magic Pickle and Jo Jo are on it!

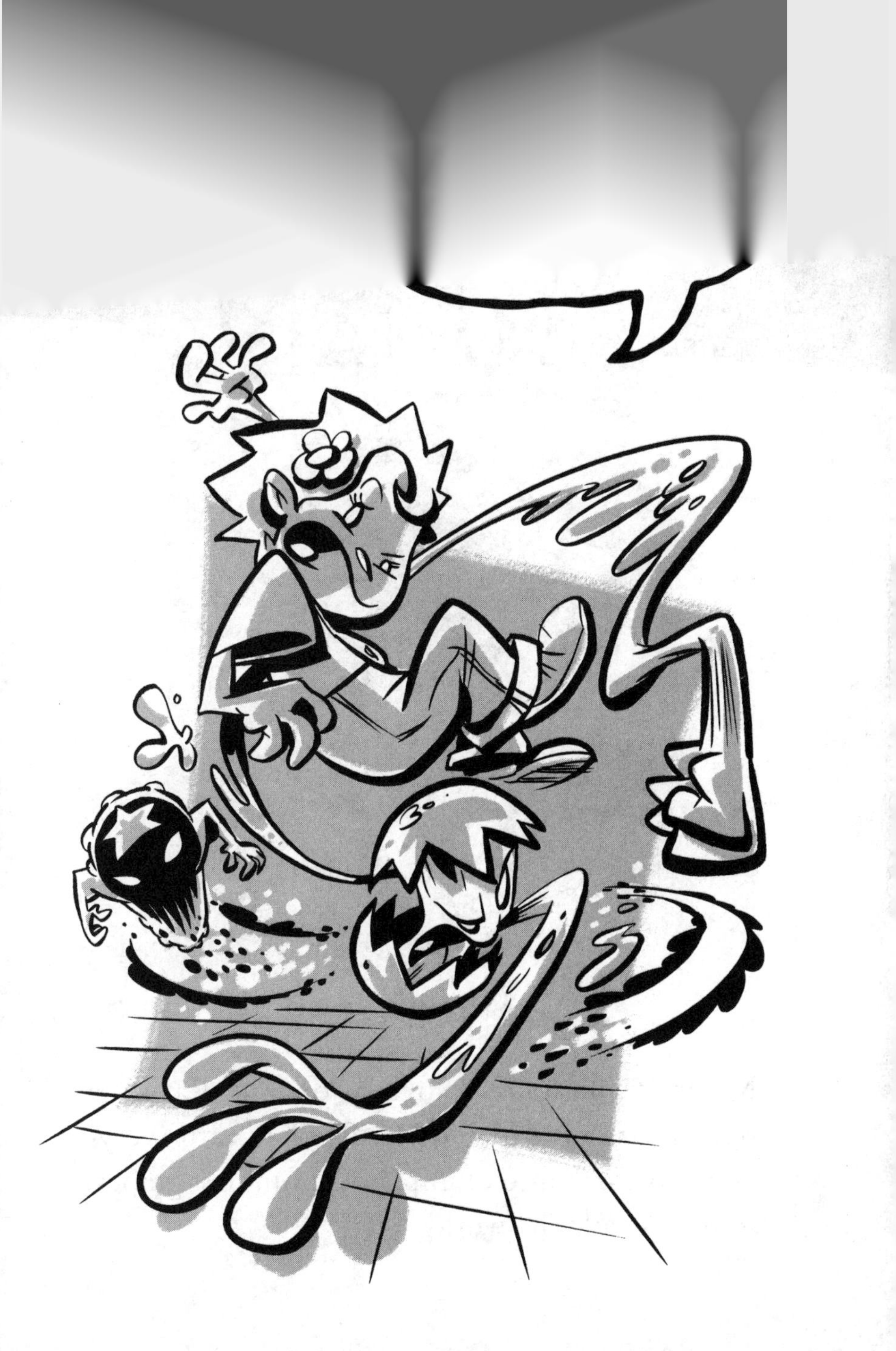

# DILL VS. DANGER

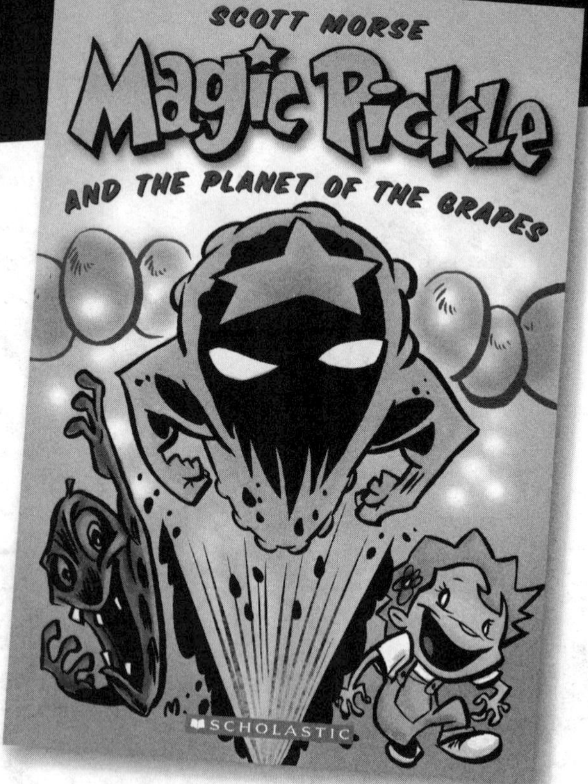
SCOTT MORSE
Magic Pickle
AND THE PLANET OF THE GRAPES
SCHOLASTIC

A graphix Chapter Book

Magic Pickle and Jo Jo take on The Razin', a renegade raisin with a dastardly plan: turn everybody on Earth into plump, juicy, mindless grapes, so he can rule the world.

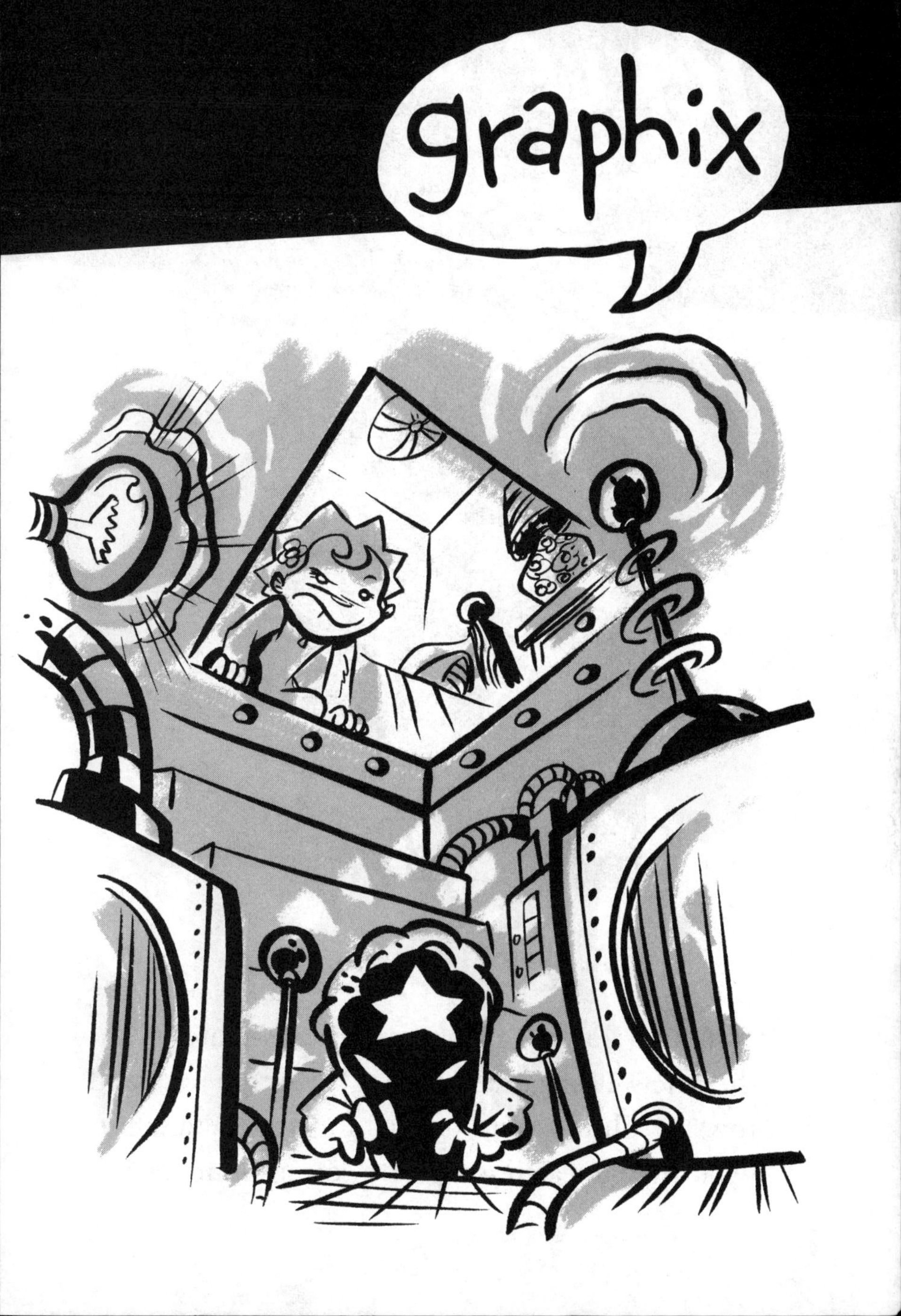
graphix

# PICKLE POWER!

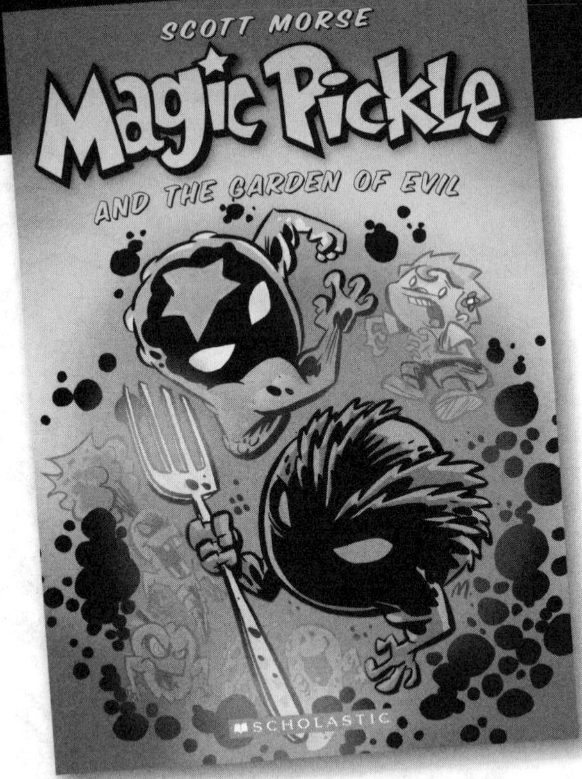
SCOTT MORSE
Magic Pickle
AND THE GARDEN OF EVIL
SCHOLASTIC

A graphix Chapter Book

When Jo Jo Wigman and her classmates plant their new class garden, they're expecting rows and rows of plump, juicy fruits and vegetables. But what they unearth is a pretty rotten bunch!

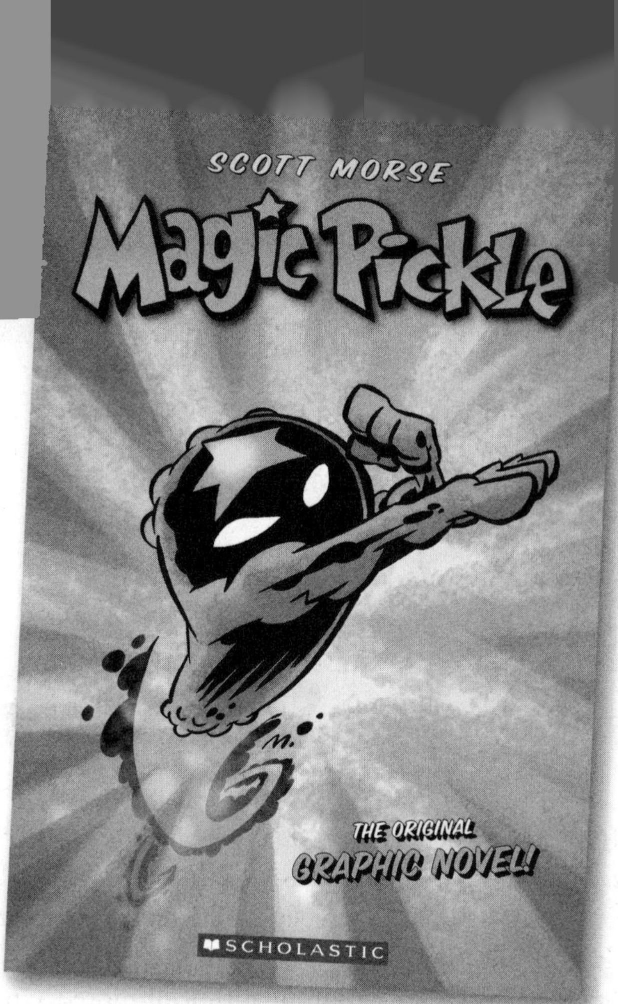
SCOTT MORSE
Magic Pickle
THE ORIGINAL
GRAPHIC NOVEL!
SCHOLASTIC

Here it is: the original **graphic novel** in full color! Read the whole story behind the world's greenest, bumpiest, briniest super flying hero, the Magic Pickle, and his feisty sidekick, Jo Jo Wigman!

A thrilling, action-packed story that starts in a secret lab and ends in a food fight!

# Meet Scott Morse

If you read Scholastic's *Goosebumps Graphix: Creepy Creatures*, you saw Scott's super-cool art in *The Abominable Snowman of Pasadena* story (and if you haven't read it, check it out!).

Scott is the award-winning author of more than ten graphic novels for children and adults, including *Soulwind*; *The Barefoot Serpent*; and *Southpaw*. He's also worked in animation for Universal, Hanna Barbera, Cartoon Network, Disney, Nickelodeon, and Pixar. Scott lives with his loving family in Oakland, California.

And sometimes—if there are any in the fridge—he even eats pickles.

# HILL COUNTRY
## COMPLETELY REVISED 3RD EDITION

Discover the wonders of Texas with
*Texas Monthly*® Guidebooks
from Gulf Publishing Company

Austin, 3rd Edition

Dallas, 2nd Edition

Hill Country, 3rd Edition

Houston, 5th Edition

Mexico, 2nd Edition

New Mexico, 3rd Edition

San Antonio, 3rd Edition

Texas, 2nd Edition

Texas Bed & Breakfast, 2nd Edition

Texas Coast and the Rio Grande Valley, 2nd Edition

Texas Parks and Campgrounds, 2nd Edition

The Texas Monthly Guidebooks

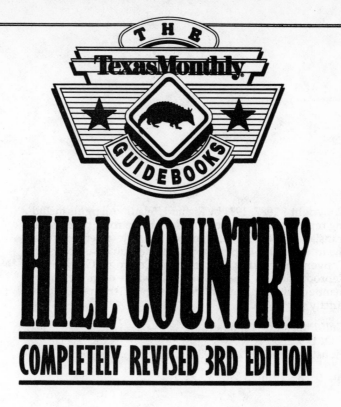

# HILL COUNTRY

## COMPLETELY REVISED 3RD EDITION

**BY RICHARD ZELADE**

Gulf Publishing Company
Houston, Texas

Gulf Publishing Company
P.O. Box 2608
Houston, Texas 77252-2608

10  9  8  7  6  5  4  3  2  1


**Library of Congress Cataloging-in-Publication Data**

Zelade, Richard, 1953–
    Hill country / by Richard Zelade.—3rd ed.
        p,        cm.—(The Texas monthly guidebooks)
    Includes index.
    **ISBN 0-87719-188-3**
    1. Texas Hill Country (Tex.) — Description and travel
— Tours.   2. Automobile travel—Texas—Texas Hill Country—Guidebooks.
I. Title.   II. Series.
F392.T47Z44      1991
917.6404'63—dc20                          91-13040
                                                CIP


Map design by Richard Balsam, Austin Boardworks.

Cover design by Hixo, Inc.

Printed in the United States of America

*Texas Monthly* is a registered trademark of Mediatex
Communications Corporation.